I0547483

Fated

Curse of the Hybrids

Book 7

LISA LAGALY

 PUBLISHING

Published in the United States of America
First Printing, 2025

ISBN
ebook: 978-1-966455-16-5
print: 978-1-966455-17-2

LL Publishing
LisaL.author@gmail.com

Recap

Honey Smith, aka Isabelle Winters, aka Guess, aka Lily has been through a lot since her parents were taken from her nearly 1.5 years ago. After being captured and adopted by wolf a pack, she discovered her magic could do more than manipulate molecules, learned of the great sacrifices her parents had made to keep her hidden and why, and managed to complete a year of college before her parents' killer captured her. She couldn't go back to college and her pack after that, but losing contact with her new friends wasn't all bad. She met her grandmother and, for the first time ever, was able to learn and study and practice her own brand of magic almost without fear of discovery. It couldn't last, but it was enough to give her the knowledge she needed to protect herself when she embarked on her quest to find the five curse tablets that would free her and the magical world from the curse of the hybrids forever.

So far she's succeeded in snagging three of the tablets. According to the book in her family's library, one of her ancestors destroyed the Wixx copy. That leaves the tablet at the bottom of the ocean. It's getting more challenging to stay ahead of all the people after her, but she's close to completing her quest. All she has to do is figure out how to retrieve something from below several miles of water and destroy any associated curses and all the tablets. After that, she'd deal with being a Celestial Luna and her apparently fated mate, if she makes it that far.

3

1

HONEY – NOVEMBER 30 – CANADA

Honey yawned and poked her head out from under the sagging bed to swivel her ears unimpeded. Someone was inside the house. She crept out of the sleeping bag and, shivering at the sudden loss of warmth, sent the bag to the nether with the tip of her tail. Being careful to avoid the creaky part of the floor, she padded to the top of the staircase and peeked down. Whoever it was hadn't made it to the steps yet. The beaded curtain she'd found elsewhere in the abandoned house and nailed up in the middle of the stairs was hanging quietly.

The musty scent of wolves wafted up the steps. Darn. She wouldn't be able to hide here anymore. Wait, she recognized that scent. A familiar furry head appeared at the bottom of the steps and looked right up at her. Tongue lolling, eyes wide with excitement, the wolf charged up the stairs and right through the beads, pulling the whole curtain down. He didn't even slow. A moment later he was all over Honey, yipping and licking and bouncing around her like a pup.

"Cede, you idiot. The floors aren't stable. You're going to bring the whole house down on top of us," a familiar voice yelled from the bottom of the stairs.

Honey transformed and pulled Cede into a hug, trying to get him to calm down. He did stop and rest his large head on his shoulder for a whole second before proceeding to swab the side of her face with his huge tongue.

She pushed him away with the dirtiest look she could conjure.

"Isabelle," Derrik called up the stairs, "can we come up?"

"You told them I was here?" Honey whispered.

Cede nodded excitedly.

"You know I'm in hiding, right?"

Cede gave her a wolfy grin.

"Are you here to kill or capture me?" Honey yelled down the stairs.

"Neither."

"What are you here for then?"

"Can't we visit as friends?"

"Am I a friend?"

"Unless you don't want to be." Derrik's head popped up above the level of the floor and he sniffed. "It really is you."

"Who did you expect?"

Rock's head popped up beside Derrik's. "Is it true you're part wolf?"

Honey transformed in response, earning a strong nuzzle from Cede. She popped back and trapped him in a headlock to give his head a vigorous rub.

"I knew no normal witch could run that fast," Derrik declared, finishing his climb to the top.

"Can you do that again?" Rock asked, gaping at her from the steps. Honey cocked her eyebrow at him, transformed with her eyebrow still cocked, then transformed again before turning to Derrik. "What are you guys doing here?"

"There were reports of a motorcycle and lights around this house. Alpha Aki sent us to check it out in case it was a rogue." He sniffed at her. "You're not a rogue are you?"

"I can't be a rogue. I'm a hybrid."

Cede whined and leaned against her.

"He says he wishes he were a hybrid," Derrik said, shaking his head.

"No, you don't. People tend to want to kill hybrids."

"Not us," Rock said, finally emerging from the stairs. He plopped down onto his knees so that he was facing her. "Have you always known you were a hybrid?"

"It's kind of hard not to know."

"You knew when you were here."

"Of course."

"But you weren't a Luna then?"

"No."

"You really are?" Derrik asked, squatting next to Cede and staring at her forehead. "Take off your hat."

She tugged off the beanie and waited patiently while he scanned her forehead.

"Those are real, eh?"

"I didn't draw them on."

Cede stepped back and started to transform.

"Don't do that," Derrik admonished. "Nobody wants to see your skinny naked ass."

"It's okay. I've got extra clothes." Honey flicked her wrist and pulled Jay's tent out of the nether complete with all the spare male clothes she had.

"Wow," Rock said while she dug out a pair of sweats and a hoodie. "Now I wish I was a hybrid. We could run wherever we wanted without worrying about carrying our clothes."

Honey held the clothes out to her side without looking behind her. A few seconds later, they vanished from her hand. Cede's transformation had gotten a lot faster.

"Who's your alpha?" Derrik asked.

"You wouldn't know him."

"That guy on TV said your alpha was dead," Cede said behind her.

"What guy?" She knew she should have gone back to the library yesterday. She'd felt so tired though after all the magic she'd expended breaking the curse and transporting people around, she'd gone to Canada and found a bed as soon as Vera and Michael had portalled back to Mr. Felix. A sense of exhilaration trickled through her as it donned on her that she'd not only saved three people, she'd scored another curse tablet. She only had one more piece of the curse to collect.

"The guy who called into WTV to verify you were a Luna."

"Who called in?"

"Someone from the Little pack in Indiana," Derrik responded.

She felt Cede move to her side.

"Did he say anything else?"

"Only that at your initiation ceremony you lit up brighter than the moon itself."

"Huh." Which one of her friends had called in and why? It was probably Nathan. He'd mentioned before the

7

importance of making sure information was presented to the public with the right spin.

Cede touched her shoulder. "Did you love him?"

"Who?"

"Your alpha."

"Not romantically, no. He was nearly twice my age, but I did and do consider him a good friend."

"I was there when Alpha Aki chose our Luna. I was just a kid, but doesn't the Alpha have to be there when a Luna is presented to the moon?" Derrik asked.

"He was there – in spirit. I think I was the only one who could see him though."

What a horrible conversation to have right after she'd woken up and was shy a couple of meals. She dipped her head so the boys wouldn't see the tear crawling out of the corner of her eye. An arm pulled her to a chest that smelled like a combination of laundry detergent, Cede, and faintly of Jay.

"I'm sorry you lost your friend," Cede said. "I know what that's like."

He did. He truly did. She could smell his sincerity and sadness. That her funny go-lucky friend knew such loss made her even sadder and she gave up trying to contain her tears and let them pour out onto Cede's borrowed shirt.

"Geez Cede, you know just what to say, don't you," one of the guys said.

"It's not his fault," Honey sniffed, swiping her cheeks with her sleeve. "I'm hungry. I'll be much better after I eat."

She pulled her backpack out of the nether and started searching the pockets for a snack, keeping an eye on the three wolves at the same time. She trusted Cede not to tell anyone

8

she was there. Rock and Derrik on the other hand, were decent guys but they were much more loyal to their alpha and therefore more likely to report her.

Derrik's phone dinged. He pulled it out and started typing.

"You're not telling anyone I'm here are you?" Honey asked.

Derrik pressed one more button then held up his phone for Honey to see. She read:

Alpha Aki: Find anything?"

Me: A friend.

Another message popped up:

Alpha Aki: Isabelle?

Derrik typed *yes*.

Alpha Aki: Keep her there. I'm coming.

"Cede, can I have the clothes back? I better go." Where to though? Maybe the shed. Phooey, she was hoping for a good breakfast this morning.

Derrik typed something rapidly into his phone then held it up for Honey.

Me: We promised we wouldn't try to capture or kill her.

Alpha Aki: Tell her I just want to talk.

"Does he truly just want to talk or is he telling you that while planning to surround the house at the same time?"

"I don't know," Derrik admitted, frowning at his phone.

"Take me with you," Cede begged.

"I thought you liked your new pack."

"I'll like your pack better."

Honey leaned her forehead against his. "My pack is currently without an alpha. You need an alpha. Maybe someday, when this mess is behind me, you can join."

9

Cede threw his arms around her and squeezed her tight. "I love you."

"Jeez Cede, lay off." Rock leaned forward and pulled them apart. "Don't mind him. He tells girls he loves them at least once a week."

"I do not."

"Isabelle." Derrik held up his phone again.

Me: She doesn't trust you.

Alpha Aki: She has my word, I only want to talk.

"What about the rest of the people with him?"

Derrik immediately typed in her response, then replied, "He says his beta just wants to listen."

All she remembered about Alpha Aki was that he was big and hairy and naked, but he had given Cede a chance after she'd pleaded his case. "I guess I can wait." She unwrapped the snack bar she'd uncovered and stuffed it into her mouth, then washed it down with all the water left in her water bottle. Her stomach gurgled angrily when she didn't immediately feed it something else.

Cede stood. "I'll be right back."

"Where are you going?"

"It's a surprise."

"A good one?" she asked.

He nodded and grinned, then disappeared down the stairs in Jay's sweats and pale bare feet.

"You better go with him," Derrik said to Rock.

"Where is he going?"

"Who knows with him," Derrik replied.

Rock disappeared down the stairs too.

Honey pulled out another bar. She felt a little better but now her mouth was dry.

Downstairs, the front door creaked and wood popped, announcing Alpha Aki's arrival. That was fast. He must not have been very far away. Honey sent her tent and her pack into the nether and made sure there was nothing else laying around in case she needed to make a quick exit.

"I'm coming up."

Honey scooted closer to the stairs. There were only two people that she could see, but she froze them and Derrik, then took a quick look out of the window behind the house. She didn't see anyone or any vehicles. She slipped past Alpha Aki on the stairs and peered around Alpha Aki's beta to make sure no one else was in the room below. Only one vehicle was parked in the front and she couldn't smell anyone else. Perhaps Alpha Aki truly meant her no harm. She still searched him and his beta's pockets on her way back up the stairs. The beta had a gun which she emptied of bullets, and a taser from which she removed the batteries. Alpha Aki only had a phone which she was tempted to search to see if he'd told anyone where she was, but she'd already refroze him once. She put the phone back and ran back up the stairs to sit by Derrik before she unfroze them all.

"Where are Cede and Rock?" their alpha asked as soon as he reached the top the stairs and took a look around.

"Cede ran off like he does so I sent Rock after him."

Alpha Aki's eyes fell on her face, then flicked up to her still uncovered forehead. "Luna."

"Alpha."

"Where is the alpha who claims you?"

"I do not need an alpha's protection."

"Did you kill him?"

"No."

Alpha Aki wrinkled his nose. "I smell guilt."

"It was due to a mistake on my part that he died. I should have sent him home before trying to break the curse."

She forced back the tears and kept her head up so she could keep an eye on the two men in front of her. The beta was trying to slip unnoticed past the alpha to stand out of her sight.

"Mr. Beta, stay where you are so I can keep an eye on you please."

Alpha Aki nodded and the beta stopped, but Honey noted how the beta positioned his hand over the pocket with the gun.

"What did you want to speak to me about?"

"Will you show me your wolf?"

She knew why but she still asked, "Why?"

"Do you know what you are?"

"I do, but you must not since you're asking me to make myself vulnerable to you and your beta."

He dropped down to the floor so that his knees were folded underneath him and motioned to his beta to do the same. "Please. I have to be sure before I do this."

"Do what?"

"Pledge myself and my pack to you."

The beta's eyes didn't move from her, but his frown was clear enough. He didn't like the idea.

"Why would you do that? You're an alpha. You're basically a king."

"A Celestial Luna is higher than the alphas. Think of it like an empress or perhaps a queen above lords. As to why – the moon favors those who submit to her chosen, plus if I make a formal pledge to you as a luna I am not legally required to kill you or turn you in. You can stay with my pack as long as you need and we will protect you."

The beta's frown shifted from her to his alpha.

"That's extremely generous, although I wouldn't ask that of anyone. What do you get out of it?"

"Besides an alliance with a person who can cure rogues and break spells?"

"Yes."

"Isn't that enough?"

"That's all you want of me?"

"All?" He gave a halfhearted chuckle. "Do you know how many rogues I've had to put down in my life because there was no way to heal them? I feel like I lose a little of my soul every time. I've got two I'm holding right now that should have already been put down, but I was hoping I'd run across you again."

He hadn't quite answered her question, but what he had said sounded sincere.

"Would you expect me to join your pack?"

"No. Like I said, you're above alphas, although if you did want to join my pack I would welcome you."

The beta wrinkled his nose behind Alpha Aki's back.

"You and Cede would probably be the only ones."

Alpha Aki snorted.

Derrik elbowed her. "Hey, I wouldn't mind. Show him your wolf."

Alpha Aki started to rise. "I can g... Fudge!"

Honey winked at him in her wolf form, then transformed back into her human one.

"Fudge?" she asked.

"Luna Leia doesn't like it when he cusses. She makes him sleep in an actual doghouse," Derrik whispered loudly.

"I think I like your luna already."

Alpha Aki didn't even crack a smile. Instead he bowed over his knees until his head was on the dusty floor. "Great Luna before me, I pledge myself and my pack into your service. Our teeth are your teeth. Our claws are your claws. Our fires are your fires and our food is your food. Please accept our humble offering and deign to place your protection over my pack."

"Um..wow. There's probably something official I'm supposed to say to that but..."

The itch in her thumb that had started during Alpha Aki's speech was now starting to feel painful and hot. She lifted her hand to knock away whatever was biting her and was shocked to find her thumb lit up like a glow-stick. It felt like hands were guiding her when she reached down to lift Alpha Aki's great head far enough to place her glowing thumb in the center of his forehead.

"I accept your pledge. Receive the gift you most desire."

Even though she wasn't the one directing the molecules into the right places, she understood what was happening. The many connections in Alpha Aki's mind were strengthened and realigned to withstand the harshest of attacks. As a last touch, she added an anchor to a minuscule section of her thumb.

"There. I have…"

Something heavy hit her in the side, sending her crashing through the wooden railing around the stairs. She was so used to sending herself to the nether, that she did it on reflex while still in midair. A moment later, she popped back into the storage space in the unfinished part of the second floor where she'd placed her latest anchor. Through the thin walls, it wasn't hard at all to hear Alpha Aki yelling.

"What did you do?!"

From the limited view she had between the slats in the wall, it looked like he was yelling down the stairs.

"My job. I was protecting you!" A male voice yelled up the stairs.

"From a little girl with a glowing thumb? Gee thanks."

"She had you under her thumb for ten minutes at least. What did she do to you?"

Alpha Aki shook his head slowly. "I'm not sure. I don't feel any different."

"I strengthened your mind so you don't have to worry about accepting rogues into your pack and I made it so you can talk to me," Honey sent telepathically. *"Nod if you can hear me."*

Alpha Aki nodded and looked around. Her thumbprint shone brightly in the center of his forehead.

"It also looks like I marked you. That might fade though."

"Great Luna, please accept my apology for my beta's actions."

"She came back?" the voice called. "Derrik, protect the alpha!"

"I'm fine Derrik. Go downstairs and see if he broke anything."

Downstairs, the door creaked open again. She heard a faint "What happened?" before the mouth-watering scent of sausage and hash browns filtered up the steps and directly to her hiding place. Her stomach let out an embarrassing roar that had everyone turning her way.

"Hang on, I'm coming!" Cede called from below.

"Don't you dare go past me, you two-bit fleabag."

"Piers, let him pass."

"Alpha, you've been compromised. Let me handle this."

"I said, let him pass."

Honey didn't bow under the command, but she could tell from the way Alpha Aki swelled and the way Derrik flinched, that it was a strong one.

"And put your phone away. I made a pledge. She is under our protection. Anyone who attempts to harm or turn her in will be immediately ousted from the pack!" Alpha Aki called down the stairs before turning to her wall. "You can come out now. I promise none of us here will harm you."

Like there was any way she would say no to hash browns.

2

HONEY – A HALF-HOUR LATER – CANADA

"No, Alpha Aki," Honey said as kindly as she knew how so the big, gruff alpha didn't take her words the wrong way. "I don't need to meet your family. The fewer the people who know I've been here, the better. Just introduce me to your rogues."

"You're going to have to go through several lines of pack security to get to them. There's no way you can avoid it, so you might as well meet everyone."

"It's safer if I don't." She switched to telepathy. *"Just call me when you get there."*

"Call you?"

She tapped her head.

"Great Luna…"

"Call me Honey."

"Luna Honey, you have my pledge. No harm will come to you."

"Please understand, I've been running for my life the past four months and hiding my entire life. It will take me a while to switch gears."

After a disappointed look and a sigh which probably worked as well as his alpha power on members of his pack, he conceded with, "As you wish."

"I'll stay with her," Cede chirped.

"I guess that means we will too," Derrik sighed.

"I'll text Derrik when I'm ready for you," Alpha Aki said.

"That works. Just make sure you've got room around you."

"Why?"

"So I don't land on anyone."

"What are you going to do, fall from the sky?" Rock asked.

"Something like that."

She watched the truck carrying the alpha and his beta drive away until she couldn't see it anymore to make certain Beta Piers was gone. She wondered how long it would be before he realized his gun was empty and his taser was powerless.

"Isabelle. No, it's Honey, right?"

She turned to Cede who was watching out the window with her. "You can call me either."

"Isabelle Honey."

"Funny."

He gently put his hand over hers where it rested on the rotting window frame. "I'm so glad you're not a witch."

"I am a witch."

"But you're part wolf too."

"True."

"That means we can be together."

She looked up into his boyishly goofy face. He was still skinny, but his cheeks had filled out and he looked much healthier than when she'd first met him. "Cede, things are really complicated right now and with your looks, I bet you already have girls crushing on you."

She chose not to pay attention to Rock's snicker of denial.

Cede pulled her hand to his chest. "It doesn't matter. I've loved you since the day we met."

Bother. Why did guys do this to her, especially sweet ones that she loathed hurting? She opened her hand under his so that it was pressed flat against his chest. "Cede, you are one of the sweetest guys I know. I love you too, but as a friend, okay?"

"Can I kiss you?"

"Didn't you hear what I just said?"

"We could be friends with benefits."

She jerked her hand away. "Cede!"

"Not that benefit, although I wouldn't mind."

"No."

Rock grabbed Cede's ear and pulled him away. "Come on Lover boy. Sorry about the Isabelle Honey. He's an idiot."

"Does he proposition girls often?"

"No," Cede claimed, finally managing to free his ear from Rock's tight pinch. "Only you."

"Well, that's good, I guess."

"*Honey, awake?*"

Her stomach did a little flip at Brayton's voice in her head. She shouldn't have eaten that last hash brown.

"*Yes. Is something wrong?*"

"*No. No word since yesterday. I was…concerned.*"

"*Everything's fine. I've got company though so I have to go.*"

"*Good or bad?*"

"*Good. I'll tell you later.*"

"*Okay.*"

Wait a minute. "*Your words are coming out right!*"

"*Only like this.*"

"*Still, it's an improvement.*"

"Isabelle, what's wrong? Isabelle?"

She blinked and realized the thing waving in front of her face was Cede's hand.

"I'm fine," she said, then sent, "*I have to go. I'll contact you later.*"

"*Okay.*"

"Where did you go?" Cede asked.

"What do you mean? I was here the whole time, wasn't I?" Did she flicker when she spoke to people telepathically? That would be cool, but weird.

"Yes. I meant you looked distracted."

"Oh. I was. What's been going on around here? Anything new?"

"You mean other than some girl making a chimney explode on national TV with just a wave of her hands?" Derrik snorted.

"*I* didn't make it explode. That was the spell. Did they find any more skeletons?"

"Are you kidding? The walls were loaded." Rock shivered. "How could they not smell that?"

"Did they find the bunker and the hidden room with Philomena's body?"

"Her body was there too?" Cede gaped.

"Yeah, she was somehow powering the spell with her head. I cut her off from the rest of the house with a shield spell but I don't know how long it will last."

20

She'd never seen Derrik's eyes open so wide.

"She was still alive?"

"Ish? I think part of her brain was, but her body was all shriveled."

Rock shivered again. "Let's talk about something else. The news keeps saying you've been sighted in random spots all over the world. Where have you been hiding really?"

Would it matter if she told them? Probably not. "Italy, UK, Australia, South America, India, here."

The looks on their faces! All of them were gaping at her. Rock recovered first.

"Wait, was that really you?"

"Was what really me?"

"That fight in Australia with the homeless people."

"Um, maybe. What fight are you talking about?"

He whipped out his phone. It was weird watching the fight from a viewer's standpoint.

"Oh that. Yeah. They weren't trained fighters."

"What about this?" Derrik pulled up a story about a girl who'd vanished from a cruise ship.

"No."

"This one?" Rock asked, playing a grainy video of a curvy, possibly naked girl transforming into a wolf in the moonlight on what looked like a small island in the middle of a river.

Honey gestured at her slim build. "Why would you think that's me?"

"Oh, right."

Derrik shoved his phone in front of her again with a web page titled 'The Honey Spot'. "Are any of these true?"

She scrolled down the page. The pictures in the tiny photos did look like her but, "No, I have never been sledding with penguins, nor have I wrestled an alligator. Who wrote this stuff? Wait." She scrolled back up to the picture of the ridiculous hat on top of what her hair once looked like. "That's Delilah and…" she scrolled back down. "That's Walter's car. Oh." She couldn't decide whether to laugh or cry. Her friends had made a whole web page on her, probably to lay down false leads, but in true Luca fashion, it had become something else entirely.

"Are you okay?" Cede asked.

Honey wiped the tears from her face and handed Derrik his phone. "Yes. Those are pictures of me, but my friends got creative with the photoshopping. I didn't know they'd done this for me. Oh my gosh, I miss them."

"Are these the friends you said you had when you were pretending to be a witch?" Cede asked.

"I am a witch, and yes. You might have heard of them. Nathan, Luca, Liam, and Walter. They're all sophomores at Vindale U., but Walter is a beta already and might transfer next year."

"Were those the guys you rescued last week?" Derrik inquired.

"Three of them were."

"Ooo, tell us the story," Cede begged.

She did and told them others until Alpha Aki's text came through.

"You guys have a way back, right?"

"Yeah."

"Okay, see you there."

22

Perhaps anchoring her thumb to Alpha Aki's forehead had not been the best idea. She quickly removed her hand from his face and took stock of her surroundings. She'd expected a jail at best and a dungeon at worst but this was – decent. It looked like a hospital room, albeit a very secure one complete with a reinforced glass wall. Alpha Aki's beta was glaring at her through the glass with his hand in his pocket. To her left was a bed where a woman lay strapped down under a thin hospital blanket. Beside her was a bassinet complete with a baby. Both appeared to be sleeping. The only other person in the room was a teenage boy, probably younger than her, but already nearly as tall as Alpha Aki. Aki's son she guessed, based on the boy's scent and looks.

"Babies can be rogues?" she asked, pulling the blanket down a little to get a better look at the baby's face.

"He's fine. I've already accepted him into the pack."

Honey gently touched the baby's soft cheek. His eyelids fluttered open and suddenly she was peering into some of the brightest blue eyes she'd ever seen.

"He's an alpha," she muttered in surprise, although how she knew she couldn't have said.

"Yes," Alpha Aki agreed.

"How old is he?"

"A couple of weeks."

"Who are you?" A breathy voice asked. "Where am I?"

Honey turned her focus to the mother. "I'm Honey. I'm here to help you."

"Help. Help. No one wants to help." The woman sang and rolled her head to face the ceiling.

"I do. Do I have your permission to try?"

23

The woman twisted back towards Honey with a growl. "Kill them! Kill them all!" She jerked on her restraints so hard Honey was certain she would have broken her skin if the restraints weren't padded.

"Who?"

The woman started thrashing so hard spittle was flying from her lips. Before Honey could decide if freezing her was a good idea, the woman went limp. For a second Honey thought she'd died, but then the woman gasped and sucked in a lungful of air.

This was going to take a while. She trusted Alpha Aki to an extent, but…she glanced at the boy standing next to the alpha. The man hadn't listened when she said she didn't want to be introduced to his family. No surprise really. Alphas tended not to listen.

Alpha Aki gestured toward the boy. "Luna Honey, this is Sika, my eldest and future alpha of the pack. He's here to observe."

The boy tore his eyes off the woman and focused on Honey. "Can you really help her?"

"I hope so. Where is the other rogue?" she asked, addressing Alpha Aki.

"He's in a holding cell. He's not as far gone as she is."

"Is he the father?"

"No. We didn't find them together and he's not an alpha."

She'd never thought about it before but, "Can the daughter of an alpha have an alpha son?"

"No. The power is passed through the male line, although some people believe the mother's genes determine the strength of an alpha."

"Who's the father then?"

Alpha Aki shook his head. "I don't know. From what she's said, I suspect she was raped. I'm not sure she knows who the father is."

Honey reached forward to touch the woman's head. The man guarding the door to the room shifted, making her pause. This might take hours. Would Alpha Aki stick around and keep anyone from harming her for that long? What if he walked off and Piers came by with his gun loaded again?

"Brayton, what are you doing?" she sent.

"Homework," he replied after a moment.

"Want to come and watch my back while I heal a rogue? You can bring your books."

"How thoughtful. Sure. I'll come."

"Grab your stuff. I'll pull you to me in," she looked at her watch, *"sixty seconds."*

"That's all?"

"Do you need more?"

He didn't reply.

"Why are you grinning?" Alpha Aki asked.

She shook her head and wiped the smile off her face.

Sixty seconds was a long time when you were watching a watch. She didn't dare look inside the rogue's head until Brayton was there because she knew she'd get sucked in.

"What is she waiting for?" Siku asked after about fifty seconds.

"I'm waiting for my backup. I'll be right back." She planted an anchor on the bed and threw herself into the nether. Five seconds later, according to her watch, she was back beside the bed with Brayton in her arms. His scent made her stomach act up again as she hugged him, backpack and all, to thank him for coming, but she quickly released him since Alpha Aki was standing right there.

"Alpha Aki, this is Brayton Mooney, future alpha of my former pack. Brayton, this is Alpha Aki who made a pledge to me today and his son and," she waved at the woman on the bed, "the person who needs my help."

"A pledge?" Brayton inquired toward her instead of the other alpha.

"He can explain. I'm going to get started. Give me forty-five minutes."

"Sure."

3

BRAYTON – TWENTY MINUTES LATER – WITH HONEY

Honey pulled her hands away from the woman's head with a long sigh. Brayton closed his laptop on the essay he'd been unsuccessfully trying to write and reached over to finally, finally touch her, even if it was only her arm.

"Help able to?"

She smiled over her shoulder at him. "Yes, I think so. How long did it take me?"

He checked his watch. "Minutes twenty-two."

"Wow, I'm getting faster, or her brain wasn't as stubborn as yours."

"Both probably."

"What did you do to her," Sika asked, pushing off the wall he'd been leaning against since his father left.

"The molecules in the part of her brain that allow her to speak to the pack had stopped moving and were causing a jam in her head. I made everything move again. As long as she rejoins a pack and uses them occasionally, she should be fine.

"She'll probably sleep for a while," Honey told the woman in a white coat who'd been observing from the door. "The faster she joins the pack, the better."

The woman nodded. Her eyes were more curious than suspicious unlike those of the guard next to her.

Honey ignored the guard and turned again to the boy. "Can you show me where the other patient is?"

The smile Honey flashed made her look closer to the fifteen she was than the somber young woman she'd become since last spring. Brayton ached to pull her into his arms and take her somewhere safe where she could go to school and hang out with her friends like she'd done before, but nowhere was safe.

"Sure," the surly boy smiled back.

Aaaaand she'd charmed another one.

"What did you mean when you said *his* brain wasn't as stubborn." The boy glanced past Honey to Brayton while they walked down the hall, "Did he used to be a rogue too?"

"No. He thought *I* was the rogue. A witch cursed him, but I fixed him. He's mostly good now."

"Mostly?" Brayton growled.

"Is that why he talks funny," the kid asked.

"No. I was referring to his tendency to try and alpha me around. The talking is because he's still recovering from what happened last weekend."

Brayton would have protested her accusation about the bossing, but the sentence was too complicated and she'd slipped her hand into his.

"He said you chose him. Is he your mate?"

Honey squeezed his hand. "He's my alpha."

"Isn't my dad your alpha too now?"

"I suppose so, but… it's different."

"How so?"

Brayton squeezed her hand back, willing her to tell the kid they were in a relationship, that someday they would be mates.

"He's been with me from the first," she finally said. "He was at my Luna ceremony and stood under the moon with me. We shared powers. Your dad didn't share any powers with me. I gifted him what he wished for."

"Ooohhh, so you're not dating?"

"It's hard to date when you're hiding from the world, but," she continued while Brayton seriously considered taking his hand back, "can you keep a secret?"

The boy nodded solemnly.

Honey looked behind her at the guard following them, then leaned toward Siku and whispered, "He's a really good kisser. Don't tell anyone though because I don't want people to target him any more than they already are."

Finally! Teasing words spilled out before Brayton could stop them. "Will girls think you me attack?"

"Girls, boys, witches, wolves, I'm sure there are all kinds of people who'd like a good kiss or some bait they can trap me with." She squeezed his hand tightly. "You've already suffered so much because of me. I don't want you to suffer any more."

That called for a hug, so he gave her one.

"Isabelle!" someone yelled from the end of the hallway. A moment later a scrawny boy with a big nose and a mop of hair was panting over Brayton's shoulder. Honey pulled herself out of Brayton's arms and smiled at the boy.

"Hi Cede."

"Who's this?" the boy asked, his friendly demeanor belied by the not-so-friendly look he bestowed upon Brayton.

"This is my, ah, Brayton."

"Cede, you idiot, why do have to run everywhere?" another male yelled down the hall. "Whoa, do I know you?" the second male asked, coming to a stop behind Cede.

"He was on the news last week," the third male behind the second said.

"Derrik, Rock," Honey said, pointing to each one as she spoke, "This is Brayton. He's my chosen alpha."

"What does that mean?" Derrik asked.

"It means I chose him to stand with me under the moon."

"He's your mate?" Derrik asked, looking at Brayton then back at Honey with a puzzled frown.

"No, he's..."

"hers," Brayton interrupted, throwing his arm over her shoulder. A mistake, he realized immediately, before she shrugged him off and glared.

"Brayton!"

He backed away and ducked his head. "Sorry."

She punched him. "You can't use your alpha power on my friends like that."

"What?" He glanced up and realized all the people around them had their heads down and were backing away.

"Sorry. Stop. Not still…ugh."

He transformed and tried again. *"Sorry. I'm still getting used to my new power."*

"New power?" she asked.

"Yeah. I'm stronger than grandfather now. I can command witches."

"Really?"

30

He nodded. *"And sorry for getting possessive. I know you don't like that. I just…you know how I feel."*

She dropped down on her knees and put her arms around him. "I know. *I'm still getting used to the idea, but,"* she kissed his furry cheek, *"you're growing on me."*

"Like a wart?"

She smiled big enough that her eyes smiled too. "Yeah, pretty much."

"Daamn, you're strong," Siku said to Brayton, reclaiming his position on Honey's other side.

"Better not let your mom hear you cuss," Derrik said.

"He can transform like you," the big-nosed kid said to Honey, a note of awe in his voice.

Honey stood, wiping non-existent dust off her knees from the polished floor. "Yeah. That's what happens during a Luna ceremony. Powers are shared. It's usually not obvious I think because most wolves all have the same powers."

"What power did he share with you?" Derrik asked.

She tapped her head. "I couldn't speak that way before. Now I can and I don't even have to be in wolf form."

"And he got the ability to transform with his clothes and everything? I think he got the better part of the deal," the third boy said.

"I didn't choose. The moon did," Honey said, starting down the hallway again. "Where were we going?"

Siku jogged a few paces to catch up with her. "This way."

Brayton caught up to her on the other side. He had to work to keep from wagging his tail when her hand automatically moved to rest on the top of his head.

"The holding cells are in the next building. We're going the back way cause Dad said you didn't want to be seen?"

"It's safer," Honey verified.

"No one will go against Dad's wishes."

"Siku, I believe your dad, but in my experience, the fewer the people who know where I am, the better."

"You were on TV yesterday," he pointed out.

"That was a special case."

Siku turned into a stairwell and went down. At the bottom, he pushed open a gray metal door and led them into a dark metal hallway that felt and smelled like it was underground. Twenty feet later, they came to another gray door.

"I feel like I'm in a spy movie," Honey commented while Siku typed at least ten characters into the keypad beside the door, then pressed his thumb underneath.

"I know, right," Siku grinned over his shoulder. "Dad just installed it this year."

Honey asked exactly what Brayton was wondering. "Do you have that many prisoners?"

"No. This building serves as a bunker and a safe house and we keep a lot of pack documents here as well. Come on, he's this way."

Inside, the walls were a little brighter with pale gray instead of dark, but it still felt enclosed and underground. The short hallway stopped at yet another gray door with a keypad. Beyond the door was a gray room with four decent-sized holding cells, each with a toilet and a couple of beds. The sole occupant snarled when they entered, then started pacing back and forth, growling under his breath when they moved closer. Brayton had never seen a rogue so feral.

"Do you think you can help him?" Siku asked.

Honey had already taken her hand off Brayton's head and was approaching the bars.

"*Honey?*" Brayton sent.

She put her hand out toward the beast who was now growling solely at her and said in a soft voice, "I won't hurt you. I'm here to help."

The wolf lunged, slamming into the bars with his face and shoulders. Brayton jumped. He wasn't the only one. Honey didn't though.

"Shh. It's okay."

A feeling of peace rolled over him. Honey's fingers were nearly within reach of the rogue's mouth but he knew she'd be okay. The rogue whimpered and pressed his forehead into her hand.

"Wow," somebody muttered behind him.

The kid with the big nose laid his head on Honey's back to give her a kind of hug from behind. He wouldn't hurt her, but mindful of his duty, Brayton turned around and planted himself where he could keep an eye on both the door and Honey, and the clock on the wall.

"I think she's glowing. Is she glowing?" the guy whose name he'd forgotten, asked.

She was, but Brayton let them figure it out for themselves.

"It's been a total of forty-five minutes."
"I'm almost done."

33

Ten minutes later, Honey retracted her hand from between the bars. Brayton didn't like the way she was sagging or that she was sagging in someone else's arms. He transformed and scooped her up before Alpha Aki stepped the short distance across the room.

"Is she all right?"

"She's fine," Brayton answered before Honey could. "She just needs to rest and eat something. Do you have somewhere she can lay down, not in a cell."

"Of course. There are rooms upstairs."

"I'll find her some food," the big-nosed kid said eagerly.

Brayton nodded. Of all the men in the crowded room, he trusted the goofy kid the most.

"I can walk Brayton."

He wanted to tell Honey that he liked her in his arms and that it was safer, but he helped her stand instead.

"Thank you."

He didn't know if it was the residual effects of her power or just the way she was looking at him, but he felt a wave of … something zip up his arm when she touched him that went straight to his belly and his lips. Like a magnet to metal, his lips snapped to hers. It was just a simple kiss, but he could feel her, the peace, the sadness, how tired she was. He pulled her closer and willed some of his energy to her.

"Geez," someone muttered behind him.

Right. They weren't alone. He pulled away and looked down to see if Honey had felt what he had. She smiled up at him, glowing as only she could do, except she was so bright her short, dark curls looked white. He blinked. Nope, it wasn't his magic eye, she really looked like that. The glow was already

34

fading though, but the feeling wasn't. He put his forehead against hers and thought of all the things he would tell her if he could.

She touched his cheek. "Thank you. I feel better."

He straightened so he could see her better. "Hmm?"

"*I think you shared some energy with me.*"

"Oh?"

"*You're glowing.*"

"So you are."

"Shit! I mean, shoot."

Honey's attention snapped to Alpha Aki who was looking down at his phone.

"What's wrong?"

"Looks like I have visitors."

"Who?"

"Alpha Weldon and … half his pack at least." The alpha looked up and offered Honey a stiff smile. "You'll be safe here."

His son looked down at his dad's phone. "Are those guns?"

"Guns?" Honey frowned. "Are you guys at war?"

"No, at least we weren't."

"He knows I'm here," Honey said.

"I don't see how he could."

"Someone told him."

A voice played from Alpha Aki's phone. "*I'm here as a representative of the counsel. It has been reported that you are harboring the hybrid Honey Smith. Per the law, she must be put to death. Bring her out or have your position revoked and your pack disbanded.*"

"Stay here. I'll take care of this."

35

"Leave your phone, so we can see what's going on," Honey said.

Alpha Aki gave a single nod and handed the phone to his son. "You get your mom and siblings to safety if it comes to that."

"Dad."

Honey moved across the room and put her hand on Siku's shoulder as the door shut behind his dad. "It won't come to that. I'll turn myself in first."

"Honey," Brayton protested.

He felt the 'they're going down' grin she shot over her shoulder all the way to his toes.

"Plan you have?"

"Not yet, but I will. Let's see what happens."

"He's got his witch with him," Siku said, pointing to a woman in a long skirt standing near the enemy alpha.

"His witch?" Honey asked.

"Yeah, she works for him."

"Really? Doing what?"

The boy shrugged.

"Who are those four guys all in a row?" Honey asked. "They look too young to be his betas."

"They are his sons. The youngest is in the grade above me. He's a real piece of work."

"You've met one of them," Derrick said. "Remember those guys in uniform on the bridge."

"Those jerks who tried to boss Cede around?"

"Yep, those are the ones."

Brayton closed his eyes to ward off nausea when the camera panned rapidly to the right. When he opened them again, Alpha Aki and four other men were exiting through the front gate of the compound. Aki stopped several yards from a fully bearded, short but muscular man, backed up by four taller, equally bearded and muscular men.

"Alpha Drew Weldon. How nice of you to visit."

"Where's the hybrid Aki?" the other alpha demanded.

"What do you know of the girl, Drew?"

"She's a hybrid. That's all I need to know."

"You watched the news yesterday, right? You saw her break the curse and the stars on her forehead? You know what that means, right?"

"Superstitious nonsense."

"She can heal rogues, Drew. I've seen it. In fact, I have a couple of them in my pack now."

"I wouldn't be bragging about that if I were you."

"Besides, by law, she's protected. You have no jurisdiction here."

"What are you talking about? You took the same oath I did. We are required to turn in or terminate hybrids."

"Alphas are not required to turn in their lunas."

"She's not your luna."

"I swore fealty to her. She is under my and my pack's protection." Alpha Aki waved his finger at the two long rows of armed people behind Alpha Weldon. "Are you truly willing to throw the lives of your people away to attack a highly defended territory for a girl who can vanish in the blink of an eye?"

"Shoot him," the other alpha ordered calmly

"Dad!" Siku yelled at the phone.

"I'll get him," Honey said just before she vanished from Brayton's side. A moment later, she appeared on the phone in front of Alpha Aki with her thumb on his forehead and a door at her back.

"Where'd she…" the big-nosed kid laughed. "She took the door with her."

On the phone, Honey put out her arms while holding the door up with her back. "Grab hold."

Alpha Aki didn't hesitate, but a couple of his men did. The alpha barked an order. A moment later, Honey landed in the room with the rest of them. On the phone, the door fell forward and landed in the dirt with a thud.

"Go to lock down," Aki ordered his betas.

"What will he do next?" Honey asked

"Surround us and wait for the Enforcers, most likely."

"If I leave what will happen?"

"If he does things by the book? Not much."

"They won't charge you a penalty fee?" Brayton asked.

"No. She's my luna. Legally, they can't."

"Alpha," one of the beta's interrupted, "they're getting ready to attack and the gate is opening by itself."

"Who's watching it?"

"It might be the witch," Honey said. "Get me to the gate. I'll take care of her."

"I don't think there will be time."

Honey squatted and vanished again.

Brayton grabbed Siku's arm and tilted the phone so he could see what was going on. Whoever was filming was focused on the people arranging themselves to charge the gate. Nobody was paying attention to the door still on the ground which Honey abruptly appeared on top of. She sprang up from her crouched position and, faster than humanly possible, charged right at the witch. To Brayton's surprise, she merely punched the witch in the shoulder, then sprinted toward Alpha Weldon. He was busy giving commands and never saw her coming, or perhaps he was frozen. After Honey vanished with him, the other people, including his four sons stood oddly still with their mouths stuck open in whatever words they had been saying.

Honey reappeared by the doorway with her captive. She tapped his clothes, and the middle-aged man was suddenly standing naked before them.

"Yuck," Honey complained. "Don't you people ever wear underwear?"

She vanished again. Brayton turned again to the screen. Honey didn't appear, but the witch popped out of existence. A moment later, both she and Honey appeared beside Alpha Weldon. Honey focused on the witch. From the warm honey smell of her magic, Brayton knew she was doing something, but he couldn't tell what.

After several seconds she turned to Alpha Aki who was watching and waiting while at the same time listening to the play-by-play one of his betas was giving. "I've bound her powers. When you release her, she can unbind them by saying the alphabet."

"The alphabet?"

"Yeah, I figured no one would release her on accident if I made that the release word."

"Why did you remove Alpha Weldon's clothes?"

"In case he had a gun or a knife. It was faster than searching him. I can bring them back."

"No. This is good. How long will he be frozen like that?"

"You have about ten more seconds, but I can give you more."

"Do it. Boys, put our visitors in the empty cells and lock the doors. We'll let them cool down for a while."

"Did you get the gate to shut?" Honey asked.

"Yes."

"I was right about the witch. She has telekinetic powers. Don't hold her job against her though."

"I won't. What are the Weldon boys doing now," Alpha Aki asked his son.

"They're starting to move. Looks like they just realized their dad is missing. They're calling for him. The oldest one has his phone out. It doesn't look like anyone answered. Kyle is taking off his clothes."

"He's going to try telepathy," Alpha Aki concluded.

"Want me to try and block it?" Honey asked.

"You can do that?"

"Maybe. I've never tried before."

"It won't cut him off from his pack permanently?" Alpha Aki asked.

"No. It will be like wearing a noise-canceling helmet."

"Sure. Give it a go."

Honey glanced at Brayton. *Want to be my guinea pig?*

I'd prefer to be your wolf.

She nodded like he was serious. *That will work. Talk telepathically so I can tell when I have the helmet strong enough.*

40

He obligingly popped into wolf form. *"How about a song. Happy Birthday to you. Happy Birthday to you…"*

Honey's magic surrounded him. He sang the next two lines with as much gusto as he could muster and finished with a warble. *"How was that?"*

Honey just looked at him.

"I can't hear you if you're talking." In fact, he looked at the mouths moving all around him, he couldn't hear anything. He transformed and pointed to his ear. "Nothing."

To his relief, the silence abruptly ceased.

She was grinning. *"I didn't realize you were such a good singer."*

He popped back into wolf form. *"There are a lot of things you don't know about me."*

She glanced at the still-frozen alpha for a moment, then nodded to Alpha Aki. "It's done, although he won't be able to hear you speak either."

"Let's leave then before he wakes up."

4

HONEY – CANADA

Honey pushed her fingers into the thick fur on top of Brayton's head while they followed Alpha Aki down yet another hallway. Should she go? Should she stay? She had no idea. She just knew she didn't want anyone to get hurt because of her.

Alpha Aki opened a heavy metal door coated with white paint and indicated they go through. Honey could tell from the smell there were electronics in the room, but she wasn't expecting one whole wall to be covered with computer monitors.

"This is our security center. The feed from all the cameras around the property comes here."

"Wow."

Alpha Aki chuckled. "Yeah, I know. It's a lot. A couple of my pack members are really into security. I think they binge spy movies. Brad, what do you see?"

"Movement everywhere. The deterrents are working though."

"Deterrents?" Honey asked.

"Trip wires, sudden electric shocks, booby traps basically." Brad tapped the keyboard to pull up a view of a man hanging upside down from a tree by his ankle with a wicked looking knife in his hand with which he was sawing at the line holding him. "We've caught a few."

"What happens if they get past your traps?" Honey asked.

"They reach the electric fence." Brad pointed to a fence at least twelve-foot high with coils of razor wire along the top.

"*It looks like a prison fence,*" Brayton's voice sounded in her head.

"*Your pack doesn't have one.*"

"*We don't need one. Our neighbors are friendly.*"

"Why do you have such a scary-looking fence?" Honey asked.

"Alpha Weldon is ambitious and he has four sons. His father was ambitious too. He's the reason my father never got to meet his grandchildren."

"I'm sorry to hear that."

Alpha Aki nodded.

"*Ask him what he wants out of this fight. What is his goal?*" Brayton suggested.

"Alpha Aki, what is your goal today, if you fight his pack I mean? What would you like to accomplish?"

He glanced down at her. "If I could accomplish anything?"

She nodded.

"Peace. I'd rather be allies with my neighbors than have to worry about all this," he waved his hand at the screens. "But Weldon is all about conquering and expansion."

"Is that legal?"

"The way he does it? Unfortunately, yes. He doesn't outright attack, usually. He uses scare tactics and maintains a strict no trespassing policy, so if any of my people stray into

43

his territory, they are either heavily fined or have to join his pack."

"Wow."

"And of course, if there's even a suggestion that something illegal has occurred, he's all over it. He always makes sure his neighbors are punished to the fullest extent of the law, including forfeiting territory to their neighbors."

"Why did you risk me then?"

"For the reasons I told you. Plus, you can't blame a father for wanting the best for his son, although I think I'm too late for that." He glanced at Brayton who was sitting by her side. Actually, leaning was a more apt description.

"You are hoping that with my power you can defeat him once and for all?"

"I'm not opposed."

She was a pawn who'd played right into his hands. Still, she didn't mind helping rogues.

"*Do you know anything about Alpha Weldon?*" Brayton asked.

"*Other than what I've heard, no,*" she admitted.

"*You need both sides of the story.*"

"*Hold your breath.*"

One quick visit to the nether later, they were back in the cell room where she'd planted an anchor in front of the still missing door. Alpha Weldon was now a furious wolf, pacing and growling probably due to his inability to communicate. The rogue she had healed was the exact opposite, sitting calmly on his cot fully dressed. He was older and frailer than she expected, but the smile he sent her way was genuine. He stood and limped to the bars.

"You are the one who healed me?"

44

"Yes."

"You didn't need to waste your energy on me, but I thank you."

"You're welcome."

"You're the hybrid," the dark-haired witch in the neighboring cell stated.

"Yes."

"What did you do to my powers?"

"I bound them, but it's only temporary."

"It's illegal to bind another witch's powers unless it's a punishment deemed by law."

"Oh, sorry, I didn't know."

"Give them back and I won't have it added to your already long list of crimes."

"What crimes?"

"You're a hybrid?" the old rogue interrupted.

"Yes," Honey replied.

"You look normal, well, except for the stars across your brow."

"I'm a curse breaker so the curse doesn't affect me, and the stars are recent."

"May I see your wolf?"

Honey glanced at Alpha Weldon who had started barking and growling and making a nuisance of himself by throwing himself at the bars. She could have froze him and responded yes to the old man, but the fewer the people who knew what her wolf looked like, the better. "Not here."

"I understand. What's wrong with my son-in-law anyway? I've never seen him so upset."

"He's your son-in-law?"

"Did you bind the alpha's powers too," the witch asked accusingly.

Best not to admit to anything. "If I had, how could he be in wolf form?"

"I've been out of touch for a while. Do you mind explaining what's going on," the rogue asked.

"Alpha Weldon was about to attack Alpha Aki's pack lands and I stopped him," Honey said.

"Attack?"

"Alpha Aki is harboring the hybrid and refused to turn her over," the witch accused.

Brayton's warm presence beside her was suddenly much taller. "Pledge made. Celestial."

The rogue blinked. "Well I'll be a bug on a fat frog. What kind of transformation was that?"

An instant later, Brayton was back to his furry self beside Honey again.

"Show off," she told him, then turned back to the old man. "If you're Alpha Weldon's son-in-law, how did you become a rogue?"

"Family disagreement."

"Ouch."

"Yeah, well I probably could have found another pack to take me in. I was a beta for over thirty years, but the Crescent pack is my home and he's my alpha even if we don't always agree. You said he was about to attack. I assume that means my pack is here?"

"There are a lot of wolves out there."

"My grandsons?"

"I saw four," Honey confirmed.

"How did their dad get in here?"

"Magic."

"You portalled us," the witch declared, "against our will."

"Can you portal me to my grandsons?" the old man asked.

"Can you convince them to go home and stop the attack? I'm not staying with Alpha Aki. I only came here to cure the rogues – you. I'll leave as soon as I drop you off."

"I'll do my best," he agreed.

She touched his hand where it gripped the bar and froze him just before pulling him with her into the nether.

"*Honey, wait!*"

"*Don't worry, I won't leave you,*" she sent back to Brayton just before she threw herself out of the nether again.

She landed with her fist on the door in a classic three-point superhero pose. Nobody noticed. They were all focused on the grandsons who had their backs to her and were yelling at everyone. Oh well. A moment later she had the old beta in front of her.

"Good luck," she said in his freshly unfrozen ear, just before vanishing again.

Like she'd promised, she pulled Brayton to her, then sent them both to the shed in Indiana. A wave of dizziness forced her to the ground.

"*What's wrong? Did you get shot? Where are you hurt?*"

She pushed Brayton's big furry head away from her shoulder before he could find a ticklish spot. "I'm fine. Just tired."

Brayton shivered. "*It's cold.*"

It was cold and she didn't really want to fight with her sleeping bag. "We could go to Australia."

"*How about someplace closer? Grandpa and Grandma loaned me their camper for the rest of the semester. I taped your nickle up in the storage space over the cab behind some boxes so you'd have another safe place to go to. We could go there. The heat works and I have food.*"

"You taped up my coin?"

He nodded.

"And made me a hiding place?"

He nodded again.

She threw his arms around his neck and kissed his furry cheek. "Thank you," she whispered through her emotions before dragging them both into the nether again.

5

BRAYTON – NOVEMBER 30 – INDIANA

Brayton quietly shut his computer. Still no news on Honey's appearance in Canada. Hopefully that was a good thing. He resisted the urge, again, to look behind the boxes above the cab. Honey was still there. He could feel her like he could feel his own arm. She was understandably exhausted after using all that magic, but she'd been sleeping for hours. He wanted to talk with her and laugh with her and maybe even cuddle in front of a good movie. Who was he kidding? They'd never really talked or laughed or cuddled. They were here now though, together, alone. The closest camper was three slots away with a tree between them. No one was chasing them. It was the perfect opportunity. They could be normal for a while. In fact, he should make her something to eat. She was going to be hungry. He could impress her with his cooking skills. Lucky he'd bought some bacon and eggs.

Loud pounding on his camper door and a yelled, "Hey Brayton, are you in there?" ripped all the pleasant thoughts right out of his head.

He rapidly slid out from under the too-small fold-down table and lunged across the short space to wrench open the door and glare.

Malcolm blinked innocently at him behind his raised fist. "What?"

Brayton waved his arms at the neighbors. "Wake everyone!"

Malcolm rolled his eyes. "It's 7 pm dude. Just 'cause you're sleeping in your grandpa's camper doesn't mean you have to go to bed when he does."

Cici sniffed the air then cocked her head at him. "Are we…interrupting something?"

"No."

"Is everything okay Brayton?"

"Fine!" he said loudly, and gave all three of them a glare for good measure before stepping aside so they could come in.

"Should I leave?"

"No."

Malcolm paused with his rear over the driver's seat. "What? Am I not supposed to sit here?"

Brayton waved him down.

"Where is she?" Cici asked. "Did you stuff her in the closet?"

"No. She's…"

Something soft brushed his lips. He grabbed Honey and tugged her closer to give her a proper kiss.

"Should we come back?" Rhys asked.

Honey pulled away from Brayton and turned so that her back was against the small counter. "No. I'll leave."

"No. Cooking I'm."

"Really? What are we having?" Malcolm asked.

"Not you for."

50

"Are you guys getting the impression that he doesn't want us here," Cici asked, "because I am, despite that we drove all this way just to see him."

"One mile?" Brayton asked.

"Hey, it was a busy mile and Malcolm was driving," Cici huffed.

"Ah."

"Did you guys eat yet?" Honey asked.

"No," Rhys said, "The cafeteria doesn't reopen until Monday. We thought we'd come here and share some pizza with our future alpha."

"Oh that's…" Honey started.

"And our Luna."

Honey looked toward the door, then turned to peer out the window even though Rhys was staring intently at her. "Luna Lynn is here?"

"You are Brayton's Luna, so you're ours too."

"What about Luna Lynn?"

"We can have more than one Luna."

"But we're not…" she turned her big green eyes on Brayton, "…not yet and…"

"Honey, you're a Luna," Rhys said calmly, "there's no changing that, and you joined our pack first. To me, you will always be our Luna."

Honey turned her attention back toward Rhys where he was leaning on the very narrow piece of wall between the kitchen dining set and the driver's seat. "That has got to be the most I've ever heard you say and also the sweetest. Thank you."

"Plus," he waved his finger at his forehead, "you're the only one I know with three spots so yeah, I'm going to claim you."

"Ditto that," Malcolm said, pulling out his phone, "what kind of pizza do we want?"

It was the first time Brayton could remember that he'd eaten with just Honey and his friends outside of the pack. All three of his betas were cracking jokes and fooling around like they always did. It was just the kind of ridiculousness that Honey's friends got up to, but the longer the evening went on, the quieter and more distracted she became.

He elbowed her gently. "Honey. Wrong what?"

"Nothing."

"Quiet you are."

She shrugged.

"Yourself you..." he started. It was never going to work. He put the rest of his pizza down and transformed.

"Remember when you told me you couldn't be yourself," he sent.

She looked at him. "Yeah."

"Well now you can. We all know what you are and we don't care."

"You don't care, but that doesn't mean your friends agree. I spoke with Alpha Aki while we were waiting for the pizza. It was his beta, well his beta's wife, who reported to the other alpha that I was there."

"Did everything work out all right?"

"Yeah. Alpha Aki released Alpha Weldon and the witch and everyone went home."

"What about the old rogue?"

"I think he went with the Crescent pack."

"My betas aren't like that."

"You don't know that. They might be secretly resenting me. They could have already texted your mom."

"They wouldn't."

"Ask them."

"I don't need to."

Honey sighed and put her half-eaten piece of pizza on the greasy paper plate in front of her. "You three, tell me the truth, okay. Are you going to tell anyone that you saw me here?"

Rhys, at least, shook his head.

Malcolm shrugged, "No one who would care."

"What do you mean?"

"If they asked me, I'd tell your Little friends and alphas Brandon and Braxton, but I'm not going to go around and blab. People might come after Brayton again."

Honey nodded and looked at Cici.

"If I thought it wouldn't bring harm to Brayton or hurt our pack I would tell someone."

Honey nodded like she'd expected Cici's answer. Brayton was too shocked to think how to respond.

"It's nothing against you as a person," Cici continued. "It's just dangerous to be associated with you and you aren't the right Luna for him."

"Why do you say that?"

"You're a hybrid. Hybrids, at least in the animal world, have difficulty having children. He needs a son at some point and his family has traditionally only managed one son each generation."

"Managed? You mean they didn't do it on purpose? I figured it was their way of avoiding fights like the Meyers."

"No, I know for a fact that Brayton's parents were trying for more kids. I heard my mom and Luna Lynn talking about it."

"Yeah, I could see why she'd want to try again," Malcolm quipped.

"Ha Ha," Brayton sent telepathically to everyone in the trailer.

"I am also concerned about Brayton's safety," Honey said, ignoring Malcolm completely. "I don't plan to stay here. Today was a one-off. Are one of you planning to stay with him?"

"No," Brayton projected to all of them.

"We're going to take turns." Cici replied as if he hadn't spoken. "Rhys was going to stay tonight, I'll take tomorrow, and Malcolm has the night after that unless Alpha Braxton decides to take a turn. I think his dad has assigned some guards to watch the trailer too."

"Good."

"I didn't agree to any of that," Brayton protested.

Honey pushed her hand into the fur on top of his head and started rubbing the sweet spot behind his left ear. "You didn't have to. You are their future alpha. Of course your pack will protect you, as they should." She kissed his cheek. "Thank you for letting me rest here a while and for the pizza. Stay safe and ace your finals. *I'll call you later.*"

"Honey."

It was too late. Her seat was already empty.

6

HONEY – DECEMBER 8 – CANADA

Seek-it spell: Can lead the user to objects associated or related to another object or person from great distances. Considered more advanced than the find-it spell which only points in the right direction.

- *School*: Divination.
- *Pros*: With the right artifact it can be performed by a witch in any branch of magic.
- *Cons*: Dangerous. People and animals spelled to seek something out cannot do anything but seek. Do not attempt to seek with living things.

"That's it! Ow."

Honey rubbed the top of her head and peered around in the dark library to see if anyone had noticed her outburst or the bang from her head hitting the underside of the table. Since it was the middle of the night and her table was far away from the entrance and the front desk, she wasn't surprised that the rest of the library remained silent.

"Where can I find the incantation for this seek-it spell?" she whispered to the innocuous-looking notebook she'd borrowed from the front desk.

At least twenty neatly printed call numbers appeared on the open page under the weak light provided by her tiny flashlight.

"You are wonderful," she told the book in lieu of 'thank you' because she didn't want the list to disappear just yet.

More characters appeared next to the numbers. Restricted access, but that didn't matter because both books owned by this library were on loan. The rest were in other libraries, all restricted. She slumped in disappointment.

"It couldn't just be easy, could it?"

"*No*," the book spelled out on top of the list.

Not for the first time, she wondered who had made the notebook and if the librarians ever had conversations with it.

She jotted down the more promising-looking titles then asked, "Are there any books currently available in this library that will tell me more about the seek-it spell and things I need to know before using it?"

The notebook obligingly listed three.

"*When Spells Go Wrong*?" she read from the top of the list. "You suggest that one so often I'm beginning to think you wrote it, or your maker did at least."

The notebook didn't respond.

"It's a good book. I might purchase it for myself someday if I ever have a place to live."

The notebook responded with another title.

"*How to Build A Mobile Home* by Baba Yaga," Honey read. "You're kidding. I thought she was a fairy tale character."

She could have sworn the notebook shrugged, but it could have been a trick of her unsteady light.

"I'll jot it down and take a look when I have a chance. Tha...You are very helpful. I don't suppose you can tell me how one gets permission to read restricted books?"

The notebook spit out another line of writing.

"Really? There's a whole book of laws about libraries? I'll put it on my list. What about an artifact that can be used to retrieve lost things? Where would that be located or what book should I look in?"

To her surprise, a book title didn't appear on the page, just a single line with a name and address.

"The Boston Library? You're kidding. There's only one artifact and it's there? Is it on display or is it restricted too?"

The notebook didn't reply.

It was for the best. It wouldn't be safe for her to go there. They'd probably upped security since her last visit. She did still have the disguise charm her grandmother's future-seeing friend had given her specifically for a trip to Boston which she hadn't used the last time. Maybe she was supposed to go to Boston again.

She was getting ahead of herself. She hadn't even finished skimming the spell dictionary yet. There might be something better she could try.

Hours later, back aching from her cramped position and eyes watering from reading so long, Honey finally had to concede that although there were a few options, like the associate retrieval spell, there wasn't anything that would work better than the artifact.

"Honey, are you awake? Are you there?"

Brayton's voice made her jump, but she managed not to whack her head again. Why was he calling her at 2 am? *"Brayton. I'm here. Is something wrong?"*

"The news. Some girl who looked just like you was shot and killed when she tried to rob a magic store."

"I have never robbed anyone." She almost said 'would' never, but she'd done all kinds of things in the last few months she'd never imagined doing.

"I know. I'm glad it wasn't you."

"Why are you up so late, or early?"

"Mom called to see if I was here. I guess she was afraid I'd be with you."

"Why was she up so early?"

"I don't know. What are you doing? Did I wake you?"

"Nope. Doing research. I think I found a spell I can use if Vera doesn't figure hers out."

"Really?"

"Yeah. I just have to locate an artifact. Actually, you could help me. Could you ask my grandmother in private, if she has a seek-it artifact?"

"Sure. Are you going to bed soon? You could stay here. Rhys is staying with me tonight. He won't tell anyone."

"Tempting, but I have a few more things to look up before I leave."

"Did you find someplace warm to stay this time?"

"I did." It was nice and warm in the boiler room at the college, just very dark and webby.

"I miss you."

A thrill went through her even though he said it every time. *"I miss you too,"* she sent truthfully.

Tomorrow, or technically, today, was Sunday, a day of rest. She never thought she'd get tired of a library, but after spending nearly every waking hour in one for a week, she needed a break.

The sun was already bright overhead when she emerged from the boiler room in full winter gear, her long blond wig, and a long skirt over her sweats. London was just like she remembered it except colder, but more colorful with all the Christmas decorations. The park near the school even had a free ice rink. After stopping by the church she'd attended in the summer to warm up and light a candle for her parents, she made her way to the mall for some cheap yet delicious Chinese food, emptying out another cash card in the process. She'd need more money soon. How stupid would it be to find a job in London where so many people knew her? Did jobs even exist where she could earn cash by the day without giving up a bunch of information? Maybe she could open a booth in that witch mall and sell protection charms, ones that worked against hybrid curses. She snorted into her rice.

"What are you laughing at," a random passing, beefy young woman snarled. Probably human, Honey guessed, since she wasn't a wolf and smelled and looked like she'd been to a gym. Honey had yet to meet a witch who enjoyed exercise, except her mother.

"Myself mostly."

The woman slammed her hands down on the table, making Honey's tray jump and the two girls with her titter. "I don't like you."

"Okay."

"You're ugly."

"Okay."

"I could pound you into the floor."

"Okay."

The girl snatched Honey's fortune-cookie off the tray. "And I'll take this."

"Okay."

The girl reached for the back of the tray again. Guessing what she was going to do, Honey grabbed her plate of food and slid out of the way just as the tray with a couple of napkins and her empty cup flipped upside-down with a loud clatter. Heads turned all around them and at least one girl whipped out her phone.

Honey raised a nonchalant eyebrow at her fuming tormentor from the safety of the other side of the small table.

"I can't believe you tried to hit me with your tray! You should be banned from the mall. Come on girls. See if I eat here again!"

Honey made sure they had actually left before picking up the tray and the other bits and settling back in her seat.

"You okay?"

"I'm fine."

The chunky teenager who'd watched the whole thing from a couple of tables away started wiping down the table next to hers. "She's like the champion of the mall gym or something and I guess she thinks that makes her queen of the mall because she does that at least once a week."

"I bet she doesn't do that to anyone bigger than her."

"Nope."

"And does she always have her cheering section with her?"

"Yep."

"How does one become champion of a gym?"

"They have karate or something and have competitions. There's supposed to be one next week."

"Is there prize money?"

The kid curled his lip. "Probably. There's a lot of them that show up. They always leave a big mess."

She couldn't compete for the money because that was just wrong to take it from some hard-working human, but it would be nice to go to a gym for a day. She hadn't been on the mat in a long time. First though, "Do you know of anyone who is hiring temporarily for the holidays and would pay cash?"

"Maybe at the park?"

"Thanks."

She finished her food, then headed for the bathroom. If she was going to stop by the gym she needed another disguise.

The small bathroom she'd discovered one day near the mall library was nearly empty. Honey slipped into the far stall before whoever was in the middle one could see her and quickly divested herself of the skirt, coat, glasses, and wig. She added a beanie to hide her stars and exchanged her baggy sweats for yoga pants. She heard the door open while she was in the stall but assumed it was the other person leaving. When she stepped out however, the bully and her two cheerleaders were waiting.

Would they recognize her? She did her best to act like they were complete strangers and pushed passed them to get to the sink. The bully ignored her and stalked to the stall she'd just vacated to throw open the door. Honey quickly rinsed her hands and wiped her face in case she'd missed something with her napkin. She'd just put her hand on the exit door to push it open when her head felt abruptly colder. She turned and gave her best puzzled frown at the bully while holding her hand over her forehead just in case humans could see her stars too.

"Why did you take my hat?"

The girl's lips raised in a kind of snarl as she held it to her nose, then out to the side as if it were a dead rat or something equally disgusting. "When did you last wash this? It stinks."

Honey knew for a fact it did not stink since she'd just washed it at Rosemary's not long ago. Why was this girl so belligerent?

"What is your problem? I saw you picking on that blond girl in the food court and now you're trying to pick a fight with me."

"You're my problem."

Honey noticed for the first time that both of the cheerleaders had phones in their hands. Shoot. She turned her back on the three of them and froze them, then ducked so she was hopefully below what the cameras could see and grabbed their cameras. It took her almost the entire thirty seconds to delete all the footage she found of herself, which was oddly a lot. They'd been stalking her almost since she entered the mall. Maybe she'd dressed too differently.

She froze them again to give herself time to get away. Abruptly, she experienced a strong tug toward the wall. It felt like her insides were trying to escape out her back.

"What in the…"

It happened again, more violently.

She threw a shield up around herself and turned to see what was going on. The wall looked like a wall, but it smelled like a sulfurous portal, a bloody sulfurous portal with ropes. With her magic sight she saw red tendrils reaching out, searching for something. She sniffed. The tendrils not only smelled like blood they smelled like *her* blood. This must be that summoning spell she'd read of in the dictionary. How had they gotten her blood?

The tendrils made a grab for her but couldn't get through her shield. How long would this go on? Would the blood eventually be spent, or did she need to make another protection charm? Would they be able to find her even if they couldn't grab her? She needed a library.

More tendrils came through the wall. If they worked together, they'd be able to grab her, shield and all. She couldn't stand here all day, nor could she wander around with full shields. That would definitely attract someone's attention. She gave herself the tiniest poke and smeared a little blood on the floor under her shield, then made a second shield around herself inside the first and sent it and herself to the nether. If she was lucky, her drop of blood would keep the spell busy and it wouldn't be able to follow her to the nether.

The problem was what do once she got to the nether. She didn't have enough time or the fresh ingredients she needed to make a blocking charm, nor was she sure how to do it. Plus, she'd never read anything on blood magic which she was pretty sure the spell was. She needed a library, but none of the four she knew of were at a distance that would make it difficult for whoever was performing the spell to find her, if distance was even a factor.

Maybe if she stayed in the nether long enough, whoever it was would use up all the blood. If she could hold her breath for a minute, about eighty minutes would pass on Earth. Yeah, they probably had enough to search for her for days, if they were using that vial of blood she'd donated. Speaking of...

"Brayton, someone is trying to use my blood against me. Do you know what happened to that blood I donated?"

A couple of minutes probably passed, but for her, his response was almost instantaneous and even sounded like it was on the same time scale. Magic was cool. *"I'll make some calls. You okay?"*

"Yeah."

Okay, What were her options? 1. Try to run. She could go to Australia or South Africa. They might be far enough away the spell couldn't reach her, although she doubted it since witches could purportedly summon demons who theoretically, resided in hell. Hell was another dimension, wasn't it. Did that mean they could also find her in the nether? Ugh. 2. Find a library. The problem was, all the ones she knew of were currently occupied with lots of witches since it was daytime, or it had been dismantled and was probably stored somewhere she didn't have access to. 3. Let the spell take her. That would be one way to see who she was dealing with. Could a summoning circle hold her? What if they had a firing squad waiting?

"Honey, it's the witch counsel. They confiscated your blood from the scientist. I'll get Dad to intervene if he can."

"No. The witches will wonder how he found out so fast. Contact my grandmother and ask her if there is a protection spell against their magic."

"Okay. Are you safe?"

64

"I can stay ahead of them, but I'd prefer not to have to run all day."

"Okay."

She'd prefer not to run at all. *"And ask how one escapes a summoning circle."*

"Are you in a summoning circle?"

"No. It's just in case."

"All right. Stay safe."

What was the witches' plan? Would they put her on trial or would they dispose of her on the spot? They had to know by now that the surest way to incapacitate her was with drugs or bullets or knives. What she needed was some physical protection, like Alpha Aki's door.

Handily, she was currently floating in what was basically a large junk yard. She called her backpack to her and pulled out her flashlight. An almost scream and a frantic kick to get away used up her remaining air when the feeble light revealed a wooden face floating right in front of her own. Was that thing always there?

She needed air. She sent herself to the campsite in Australia and after several long breaths to calm herself and empty her lungs of spent air, she realized the answer was right in front of her face, well, across the field anyway. The old school bus rusting under the trees would be perfect if its sides were as thick as she suspected. She had to hurry though. Already her shield was nearly covered with the red tendrils.

She transformed and ran, sloughing off a layer of her shield to keep the tendrils busy. It worked for all of a millisecond. The summoning spell was strong, and it seemed to be coming from multiple directions. How many summoning circles did they have? She tried to dodge the

65

tendrils, but that was pretty much useless. She wasn't going to make it to the bus. She stopped and poked the tender pad of her paw, then sent herself to the nether the way she had before.

She expected the face this time, but it was still disturbing the way it was there, staring at her, like it was waiting for something. Maybe it was. Keeping it in the corner of her vision just in case, Honey slowly scanned the nether with the flashlight in her now human hand. Her light was too weak to see much of anything and all that running had used up most of her air. She turned back to the wooden woman.

"I don't suppose you know where something big is, in case they pull me in to a summoning circle?" she sent telepathically.

To her surprise, the woman did a slow turn toward Honey's right. It did look a little darker there, maybe. Honey propelled herself forward with a few kicks. There was definitely something there, something huge, something wooden like the women. Honey reached out and planted an anchor.

"I'll be right back. I need more air, but thank you," she sent to the wooden woman.

This time she sent herself to Arthur Helman's spare bedroom, shields already up. She suspected wherever she went would be compromised and she'd never be able to go there again, but the Enforcers already knew about his place. As she expected, there were already spells in place in his house, but they were easy enough to get through.

It would have been nice to check on the old man, but the tendrils found her almost immediately. She filled her lungs and left.

The woman and the thing were waiting. It turned out to be a ship, one so large Honey had to climb up the side to get in. There was a large, splintered hole in the center of the deck and scattered about the deck...was that gold? She picked up a thick, silver-dollar-sized circle. It sure looked like it. Well, that would solve her money woes. She tucked it into her pocket.

"Honey, your grandmother isn't answering. I could ask the librarian."

"I don't trust her."

"Why?"

"She tried to drug me and freeze me to take my blood before everyone knew I was a hybrid."

"Oh."

"And if she knows what's going on and you ask her about summoning she'll know you know and then she'll know we have a way to communicate quickly. I don't want them to go after you again. Besides, I have a plan."

"What is it?"

"I found an old wooden ship in the nether. It's huge. I'll anchor my feet to it like shoes. Their summoning circle won't be big enough to contain me."

"Will that work? I mean, if you were standing in a building or in a train, it wouldn't come with you."

"I usually don't anchor them to myself."

"And what will you do once you get out of the circle?"

"Freeze everyone and get my blood back."

"What if there are twenty of them? Can you handle that many?"

"Yes." Maybe. It depended how many spells were in the way.

"What if there are more?"

"Unless there's a whole army, I should be okay."

"Take me with you."

"No. It's too dangerous."

"I can command witches. I can help."

"No Brayton."

"Honey, please. You are my Luna. I'm supposed to protect you."

"You can't protect me from this and if you're there I'll be distracted. Plus, I need you to be my back-up. You're my safety net."

"I don't want to be your safety net."

"Fine. Tell Walter and Nathan and Luca I might be dropping by shortly. I'm out of air."

"Honey!"

Ugh. Why did he always have to argue? No time now. She had to focus. She sent herself to the old house in Canada since she'd already decided to avoid going there anymore. The tendrils found her within a few breaths. This time, she let them surround her, but just as they pulled her wherever it was they were trying to take her to, she called the ship to her.

She forgot about gravity.

Stupid.

The boat landed beneath her feet like a large shoe as planned but immediately started to tilt. She made a split decision and ran down, toward the ground covered in yellow and green grass, rather than up where she'd be exposed to snipers if they were there. Witches in white robes gaped at her instead of running away from the falling sails and mast.

She hadn't considered how close people would be standing either.

There was only one thing to do.

She sent herself and the ship back to the nether and pulled out her flashlight again.

The wooden woman was slowly floating down to the deck of the ship. Honey noted for the first time the details in her clothes. The carver had even added buckles to her shoes.

"It worked, but I might have killed someone and they still have my blood. I don't suppose you know where I can find a book on blood magic?" she asked the statue.

The statue kept sinking.

"Protection magic?"

The statue stopped in front of her face and stared with her carved eyes.

"Okay then."

Honey had already compromised three of her anchor points, assuming they could detect where she landed in real time due to her blood. The boat trick had disrupted the witches' plans for now, but really, all they had to do was draw a bigger circle and try again. Her window of time to find a way to block them was shrinking rapidly, more so while she was in the nether. She had to find a way to block that spell. Praying and hoping that no one had picked up her coin from the floor of Vera's school and had dropped it under their car seat or were now carrying it in their pocket, she sent herself to Texas.

7

HONEY – DECEMBER 8 – TEXAS

Her cheek landed against a cold floor. So far so good. It even had the right dust and magic smell, but not as strong as a week ago. Her flashlight confirmed it was the magical bunker although it was eerier than before now that it was empty. Even the pillar that had held up the stairs was gone. Since the stairs were down, she assumed the Enforcers must have found and taken Philomena as well.

Turning her back on the stairs, she followed the Enforcers' trail where they had hacked through the once hidden door into a large kitchen and then down a long hallway coated with a layer of plaster dust that got thicker the farther she went. She halted at the sound of thumping ahead, like someone was dumping books into a box. Had they allowed Vera back in? Honey hid her wolf feel with the charm her grandmother had given her and her smell with an air shield and crept closer to the noise. She was almost to the doorway that separated her section of the hallway from the next when a dark, humanoid shape blocked the light pouring into the hallway from farther ahead. Honey flattened herself to the wall behind a barely noticeable door frame and hoped whoever it was didn't look down the hallway.

"How much more?" a shrill voice asked.

"About ten boxes, give or take," a male voice replied.

"Make sure you take everything."

"Yes, Ma'am."

The woman's heels thumped against the floor and her shadow darkened the carpet at Honey's feet, but quickly receded. Honey wasn't at all surprised to hear the man in the library muttering expletives under his breath the moment the woman was out of range.

Did Vera know this was happening? Honey was pretty certain the woman in the hallway was a witch and absolutely certain that she wasn't related to Vera. It would be very odd for Vera to have allowed a strange witch to touch her family library. Witches, in Honey's experience, were very protective of their libraries and private collections. Vera was hard at work trying to find a way to retrieve the last tablet for Honey. The least Honey could do was make sure the girl's library was safe so she could reopen the school when she found a place to do so.

She was about to slip down the hallway to the library door when two more bulky silhouettes filled the lit doorway ahead. Their strong, sweaty scents were all wolf.

"Back already?" the book-packer asked from inside the library.

"Not done yet?" one of his friends retorted.

"I'd like to see you pack boxes in this stench."

Unsurprisingly, the book-packer must be a wolf too.

"You should smell the truck. We'll have to set off some air freshener bombs."

"Do those exist?" the third, younger sounding male asked.

"It's just a short trip. You'll live," the one beside him rumbled.

71

"Through a portal. Make sure she agrees to portal us back before you go. I don't trust that b-witch any farther than, well, at all," the voice inside the library said.

"You ever been to Boston," the younger voice asked.

"Once, but I doubt we'll have time to sightsee. She wants these unpacked tonight."

"Unpacked on the shelves unpacked?" the younger voice squeaked.

"No. Just stacked. Witches don't allow no wolves in their sacred libraries."

"Except this one."

"Yeah."

Boston? Witch library? It was too good to be true. That didn't mean she wasn't going to take advantage of it. After a quick glance at the front door to make sure no one else was coming, Honey froze the three wolves and quickly slipped into the room.

The previously cozy library was a disaster. Two walls and half of another were down to the studs and chunks of plaster were everywhere. The remaining shelves were mostly empty, but piles of books remained leaning against the one whole wall. She quickly scanned all the books she could see, including the ones in the box the man was packing, for the one book she knew would have information on protections spells, but it wasn't there. That was fine. There were plenty of books in Boston. She just needed to plant an anchor somewhere. The problem was, where? She had no way of knowing which boxes were going to end up on top in the truck. She would have to come back when they were almost done. Unless…she peered out into the hallway, then made a break for the door.

Planting an anchor on the inside top of the truck door had worked beautifully. During the short trip, she sent all the boxes to the nether, then made a hole with her magic so she could stick her finger up to the top of the roof and plant yet another anchor on top of the outside of the van. Once the van stopped and the engine quieted, she made half the floor disappear and planted yet another anchor on the cement below in case she didn't get a chance to leave the van. After she put the floor back, she followed her first anchor to the nether and back to the top of the van. She materialized just in time to hear the shrill witch lay into the wolves about the missing books.

Honey felt sorry for them. They likely wouldn't get paid, but that would be much less painful than what Vera would go through if she didn't get her library back. Honey was certain that if the books were unloaded in Boston, Vera would never see them again.

"You signed a contract! If you don't deliver those books your company is done. Your whole pack is done."

"Look lady. You saw us put the boxes in the truck. You were behind us the entire way. You know we didn't stop. You were the one who insisted we use a portal. It's not our fault your portal was faulty."

"That portal was not faulty! People use them all the time. No one has ever lost so much as a fingernail. I demand you unload the books."

"Sure. We'll unload these invisible books for you right

now. Where would you like them?"

"Invisible?"

The woman's footsteps clumped closer and Honey imagined her sticking her arm inside and feeling around the van.

"There's nothing in there. Stupid wolves. You can drive back for all I care."

"We had a contract."

"Which you broke."

"Are you sure those books didn't have a homing spell on them or something," the younger wolf asked. "It seems like something that Philomena person would do."

"There's no such thing!" the woman snapped.

"Yeah there is. I saw it on Yo-Wo."

The boy wasn't wrong. Honey had read about it herself in a book somewhere. Too bad she didn't know how to actually do the spell. That would be the perfect way to protect the books without getting the wolves into trouble.

"Can't you scan the truck for magical residue or something," one of the older wolves asked. "I know you witches can do that sort of thing."

"Only a few witches specialize in that skill. They don't have time to go looking around trucks emptied by wolf incompetence."

"We are not incompetent and you know it," one of the older wolves growled. "Stop trying to blame your failure to magically protect your haul on us. We packed up everything per the contract and would gladly unload it if were here."

"Ms. Payne! I didn't expect to see you here so late. Is there a problem?" yet another male voice asked jovially, although there was an undercurrent of something harsher in his tone. Honey was tempted to flip around and try peering over the back edge of the truck to see if he looked like what she imagined but she knew the wolves would hear her.

"Monsieur Murik!" the shrill woman squeaked. "I did not expect you so late either."

"Trying to sneak another 'collection' in under my nose so you can expand your personal library?"

"No! Never!"

Honey could smell the stench of the woman's lie from the top of the truck.

"What were you supposed to deliver?" Monsieur Murik asked, making Honey wonder if he'd been listening the whole time.

"Load of books from that Texas school with the serial killer," one of the deeper wolf voices replied.

"The Lambert collection. Ms. Payne, you know we can't take anything without the council's approval."

"It is our duty as custodians of magical literature and history to see that the collection is protected. Ms. Lambert has abandoned the school. There was nothing preventing even a human from walking in and taking things."

"Other than the magical caution tape all around the building you mean," Monsieur Murik said.

The woman huffed. "That didn't even phase these incompetent buffoons."

"What magical caution tape? We were told this was sanctioned by the court. We have the written approval right here."

One of the wolves, based on the tread, stomped to the front of the truck and dug around in the cab before returning with what Honey could only imagine was a sheet of paper with a big stamp of approval. After a shorter pause than she expected, Monsieur Murik clucked his tongue and said, "Ms. Payne you have been naughty indeed."

"Naughty! The courts ordered that all dangerous items be removed. Can you imagine what would happen if those magic books had fallen into Normal hands?"

"Nothing, since Normals can't do magic. Gentlemen, I'm sorry for wasting your time. Ms. Payne, pay the men and send them back home as your contract states."

"But they didn't deliver the books!"

"Good thing too or I might have to have you arrested for theft. I still might if those books didn't make their way back home. Did you even bother to put a tracker on them?"

"Why would I?"

"Basic acquisition protocol perhaps? Now clear out of here. We have another truck coming in tonight and I need this space."

So much for popping into the library after hours, but hey, she now had a whole collection of books to look through at her leisure. She just had to figure out where she could read them. It was too dangerous to do it at her friends' houses and dorms and she couldn't do it at any of the places she'd jumped to when trying to escape the summoning spell. Plus, it had to be inside and big enough to contain all the books and leave room to open them. That left the cave, the library in Canada, and … Vera's house. Not the library though. Honey shivered at the thought of all the bodies in the walls.

8

BRAYTON – DECEMBER 8 – INDIANA

"*The attempted summoning of the hybrid Honey Smith, who is believed to be the cause of a string of bad luck experienced by people all over the world, was a spectacular failure today, and I mean that literally. The fifteen-year-old outwitted her would-be captors by somehow bringing what is believed to be a pirate ship with her into the summoning circle, shown here in this footage submitted by an anonymous viewer. Miss Smith can be seen briefly where the arrow is pointing, then the ship begins to tip and she goes out of view. The video shows people running and falling while the ship topples, but so far, no injuries or fatalities have been reported. To my knowledge, no one has ever brought a ship with them to a summoning. Because the ship was bigger than the summoning circle, Miss Smith was able to break the confines of the circle and again escape capture, taking the ship with her. No word on which organization was responsible for this attempt, but Dr. Naomi Davis, who had obtained samples of Miss Smith's blood for use in her research on curses has confirmed her samples were confiscated by the witch counsel and could have been used in the summoning attempt. Sources say not only did Miss Smith manage to evade capture, it took over two hours to pull her into the circle, an impressive feat by itself. Where she acquired the ship is currently a mystery. Madame Adelia Wixx, head of the Wixx family, and Mrs. Rachel Wixx, Madame Wixx's daughter and Miss Smith's grandmother, have been taken in for questioning.*"

"Can't say the girl doesn't have style. A pirate ship. Epic," Malcolm said, snagging another buffalo wing. "Where did she find it?"

"In one of her hiding places, I assume," Brayton replied, sniffing at the wing in his hand in a lame attempt to pretend he was hungry. At least now he knew why Mrs. Wixx hadn't called him back.

"You know," Cici said.

It was a statement, not a question.

"Yes."

"She could have killed someone. She might have."

He let the wing drop back onto his plate. "They were going to kill her and she didn't have much time."

"What are you talking about?"

Rhys turned the laptop towards Cici and moved the play time indicator back to the beginning. "Look behind the witches. Those are enforcers in full riot gear."

"No, I meant what do you mean she didn't have much time?"

Brayton nodded at the screen. "Look at all the witches around that circle. All of them are using their powers against her at once. Basically, it's one against..." he counted, "twelve. She had to continuously stay ahead of them while she came up with a plan to defeat them without really knowing how the spell works."

Cici glared across the small table at him. "How do you know?"

"Because she asked for my help."

"And did you help her?"

He sighed down at his plate. "No. I was completely useless," and he didn't know if the witches had successfully tried again because other than a frustrated 'I'm okay' hours ago, now Honey wouldn't even talk to him, but Cici didn't need to know that.

"They're witches. Of course you were useless," Rhys said.

"He could have bitten them," Malcolm quipped.

Cici threw a bone at him. "You want him to start a war?"

Brayton dropped his fist firmly on the fold-down table, but not too firmly. His grandpa had already broken it at least twice. "We need to prevent it from happening again. They shouldn't have stolen her blood."

"They didn't steal it," Cici said. "They acquired it legally and you'd be all for it if it was to catch someone other than Honey."

"I'd be for it if she was a criminal, but she's not. She's innocent of everything but having mixed blood. She was planning on taking her blood from them but she didn't because she didn't want anyone to get hurt."

"How do you know? Did she tell you?"

"No. I know Honey."

"She probably didn't want to fall off the boat right into the Enforcer's hands."

Cici was wrong.

He would have argued but, "It doesn't matter. We just need to prevent it from happening again. She can't break the curse if she's dead."

"I don't know why you're so fired up about that curse," Cici said. "The only people it affects are deviants."

"No. It affects all of us. It's probably the main reason there's so much hate and suspicion between witches and wolves."

"I found it."

Honey. Brayton immediately popped into his wolf form. *"What did you find?"*

"A way to block their spell."

He knew she would say no, but he tried anyway. *"Take me to you."*

"Why? Are you in trouble?"

"No. I want to see you. Please?"

He felt like he could burst with happiness when the darkness of the nether wrapped around him. A moment later he felt her lips, but they were on his cheek. Ouch.

He waited until they were clear of the nether then as calmly as he could, noted, "You changed your anchor."

"And you are talking normally. I'm glad." She turned away from him to weave her way through a maze of boxes toward an old, dusty wooden counter.

"Wait." He snagged her hand just before it went out of his reach and gave it a firm tug. Like he'd planned, she stumbled into his arms. "Why did you change it?"

She looked down, avoiding his eyes. "It was weird."

He forgot how young she was sometimes. Odd how when they were together, he forgot about age. All he knew and needed to know was that she was perfect for him. "No, it wasn't, but I understand. I'm the first boy you've ever kissed, aren't I?"

She ducked her head even farther. "Yes."

"And you like it?"

"Maybe."

He chuckled. "You don't have to kiss me, but I need a hug."

"You need one?" she mumbled against his chest.

"Yes. I've been worrying about you all day. I need to feel that you're safe."

"Are all alphas like this?"

He leaned into her hug with a happy sigh. "It's not just alphas."

"So where are we?" he asked after a sufficient amount of time had passed – sufficient for him that is. Honey had already tried to pull away a couple of times.

"You don't recognize it?"

"No."

"Use your nose."

He sniffed. "I smell magic and dust and...something dead?"

"Trust me," she said, trying to push away again, "it smells a lot better than it did a week ago."

"I'm not done hugging you," he said, refusing to open his arms. "A week ago? Are we at that school?"

"Yes." She leaned back against him with a tired sigh.

"Have you eaten anything today?"

"I had lunch and a couple of bars. I'm fine, just tired."

She needed more food. Why hadn't he thought to bring some wings with him? "Why don't you come back with me? I have food and you can sleep in the loft for a while."

"No. They might be able to track me with my blood. I mean, I think I did the spell right, but..." she yawned.

He pulled her closer and lay his head on top of hers. "Sleep. I'll watch over you."

"You have class tomorrow."

"No tests or homework though. Sleep. I'll use my eye. If I see anything magical happening, I'll wake you. I'm your safety net, remember? This is what safety nets do."

"Thank you, Brayton."

The gentle, lingering kiss she planted on his cheek made his insides feel like mush and induced a feeling of protectiveness that was almost painful. With difficulty, he turned the 'I love you' that wanted to spill out into 'You're welcome.'

9

BRAYTON – DECEMBER 9 – INDIANA

"Brayton. It's so good to see you. Shall we get a latte?" Mrs. Wixx asked with a kind smile.

After staying up all night keeping Honey safe and Honey's insistence that he make it to his first class, he needed something stronger than a latte, but he could address that at the register. "Sure. Thanks for getting back to me. Did the Enforcers give you any trouble?"

"No. It went about as you'd expect. They tried to use compulsion to get me to talk. Unfortunately for them, I don't know much and I have a lot of practice resisting."

"What?"

She wiggled her eyebrows at him then stepped into the line for coffee. "You didn't think only alphas could force their will on people did you?"

"Who's been forcing their will on you?" It wasn't right. He...he'd...he didn't know what he would do, but no one should force nice little old ladies to do anything, even witch ladies.

"Here's a hint. I got my healing powers from my dad."

"Your mother?!"

"I didn't say that," she said, taking a step forward in line.

"No, you didn't." Wait. Did that mean… "Your daughter was a healer too."

"Yes."

"And she had an arranged marriage, or was supposed to?"

"Yes."

"Was your marriage arranged too?"

"Yes, by my mother. I wasn't forced to marry Henry if that's what you're wondering. I knew what was expected of me, as did my daughter."

"What happened to your husband, if you don't mind me asking? Honey has never mentioned him."

"Oh, she probably doesn't know anything about him. He was an explorer. He went to South America to investigate some ruins and never came back. Her mom was three at the time."

"He disappeared?"

"Yes. He stepped into a curse, or so the people with him believed."

"I'm sorry."

She shrugged. "It was a long time ago."

Brayton couldn't imagine growing up without his dad and mom, but he knew kids had to all the time. He was lucky. He paid for their drinks and followed Mrs. Wixx to a table as far away from everyone else as it could be.

"What did they ask you about?" he asked once she'd put the anti-listening coin under a napkin in the center of the table.

She gave him an approving nod. "Oh, you know, the normal stuff. Where is Honey hiding? How do you two communicate? What is her relationship with Brayton? Where

84

did she get a ship from and how did she make it appear and disappear?"

"They must have been really irritated that you didn't know anything."

"Indeed. Do you talk to her often?"

She was shaking her head. She must be under compulsion even now.

"No." Not as often as he'd like.

"What did you want to see me about?"

Brayton didn't need her head shake to know he couldn't ask her anything important. He knew from personal experience how impossible it was to resist a compulsion spell. How could he ask about spells that would help Honey retrieve the remaining curse at the bottom of the ocean without revealing the reason?

"Oh, I was...wondering if you wanted to go in with me to get Honey a present for her birthday."

"What were you thinking?"

"I'm not sure. She seemed to really like those smoke bombs."

Mrs. Wixx chuckled. "Yes, she did. She might actually find a use for them too. How about some magical fireworks?"

"Magical fireworks? How are they different from normal fireworks?"

"They make pictures, moving scenes, and there are no-smoke and no-bang options."

"Wow."

"Some of them immerse the viewer into full illusions that last for up to a minute."

"Really? Those must be pricey."

"Not as much as you'd think. They're very popular party favors."

"I was thinking of getting her something to help her out."

Mrs. Wixx shook her head violently, but he plowed on.

"After all the time she's been running, I'm pretty sure she's probably got a sleeping bag at least and a canteen. I wonder if she has a cooking set. Do you know of any magical camping supplies she might find useful?"

Mrs. Wixx leaned back in her seat with a small sigh and took a slow sip of her coffee. "Hmm. I'll have to think about it. I can't say I've ever camped much, but there are some witches in my coven who enjoy that sort of thing. Are you throwing a party for her?"

Mrs. Wixx shook her head again. He gathered she hadn't meant to ask but didn't have a choice.

"No. I just thought if I ever saw her again, it would be nice to have a surprise ready. She'll be sixteen. My mom hinted at a big party last year but now…" He couldn't contain his own sigh. "I think it's sad that she'll be all alone on her birthday."

"Yeah. I wish I could celebrate with her just once."

The sorrow he smelled over her healing scent belied the small smile she conjured up. Brayton would have hugged her if there hadn't been a table and two hot cups of coffee between them.

"I don't suppose there's such a thing as a magical cake that pops into existence when you open a card?" he said to lighten them mood.

"I can't say that I've ever received one, but I wouldn't be surprised. How would you get it to her though?"

She was shaking her head again, so Brayton knew she didn't really want to know, but her question was exactly what he needed.

"That's the problem. I saw on TV that they were trying to summon her with blood. Can they send stuff with blood? I mean, if I had some of her blood, which I don't, could I use it to send her things or would her protection spells prevent that?"

"Without knowing what spells she has in place, I can't answer that. Do you know what she's using?"

"No, but no one has found her yet, so good ones. No one has had her blood before though."

Mrs. Wixx took another careful sip of her still steaming coffee before replying, "I am not an expert on those kind of spells, since finding and seeking spells are not in the purview of healing, but I remember something my aunt told my mother once. Realize it was a long time ago, so I may have some details wrong, but during World War II, there was a witch who developed an artifact that could send a bullet to kill a person from anywhere in the world. All he needed was something from their body. It didn't have to be blood. It could be a hair or a fingernail or even some spit. I think it must have been powered by a combination of portal and seeking spells because I don't see how a bullet, even a magical one, could zip around the Earth without hitting something else first. Thankfully, he was on our side."

"What happened to the artifact?"

"I don't know. It's probably in a warehouse somewhere."

"Then it's unlikely they'll try to use it against Honey?"

"I don't know, but Mr. Felix told me he can't portal to her, so I doubt she needs to worry about it."

Brayton took a moment to stretch and nonchalantly look around. No one was staring at them directly, but there were at least three people quite obviously *not* looking at them. He took a sip of coffee, then frowned, like he didn't understand something. "I know what a portal is, but what's a seeking spell?"

"A dangerous little spell that I have no doubt someone would use if they could ever get close enough."

"Dangerous? Why? Isn't it just used to find things?"

"Yes, but you have to be careful. Again, you need a piece of what you're looking for. You can send the piece alone or attach the piece to something and it will fly directly to what you're looking for. So, if you have some of Moby Dick's blood, for example, you wipe that blood on a harpoon, say the spell, and it will fly directly to Moby Dick. The danger is to whoever or whatever is standing between you and the whale. The harpoon will go right through any obstacles, or at least try. The spell is illegal to use without the appropriate training and a license."

"How many people are licensed to use it?"

"Not many, maybe twenty in the US."

"Only twenty?"

Mrs. Wixx shrugged. "Find-it spells work just as well and they are cheap."

Hope flared. Maybe he'd finally stumbled across a way to help Honey. "How do they work?"

"They're like compasses, but instead of pointing north, they point to what you're trying to find."

"Ah."

Nope that wouldn't work unless Honey figured out a way to walk on the ocean floor. Even the seek-it spell was iffy. She'd have to figure out how to pull the curse from the ocean floor once she found it, but at least it would give her an easy way to go directly to it, unless…

"What are you thinking?"

He shook his head. "Nothing important. Wait. Do you think they could find Honey with a find-it spell since they have her blood?"

Mrs. Wixx grinned, a full grin, which he didn't see very often.

"What?" He asked.

"Not only did Honey thwart their attempts to summon her, the ship landed on the cooler with her blood in it and totally crushed it and the vial inside. Her blood soaked right into the ground and no matter how hard the necromancers tried, it refused to come back up. They said they couldn't even feel it."

"Can they normally feel blood?"

"Necromancers can feel blood for centuries after it's been spilled."

"What do you mean feel it? What happens if they walk across a battlefield?"

"I've heard it can manifest as a tingling feeling or a smell. Sometimes they get echos of the victim's personality. It's not pleasant. Most necromancers avoid battlefields or places where lots of blood was spilled."

"Oh. I didn't realize. Why couldn't they feel Honey's blood?"

89

"Maybe Honey figured out a way to call it back to her."

"Is there a way to do that?"

"I don't know. You tell me."

Thank goodness Honey was so tight-lipped because he could honestly say, "I have no idea."

"Well, I better be going," she said, picking up the napkin with the coin wrapped inside. "Tell Honey I miss her and Happy Birthday from me if you see her."

"I will."

The caffeine helped for all of an hour. After mostly staying awake for his remaining classes, He blearily dragged himself across campus and the mile to his camper, ready to collapse on his bed for a few solid hours.

"Brayton."

He turned to the SUV he hadn't noticed and triggered another yawn.

"Mom, Bernadette," he said when he had control of his mouth again.

His mom slid out of the driver's seat and moved to stand in front of him. "I came to apologize. I lost my temper. I'm sorry."

"That's all right. I know the situation hasn't been easy on you."

He let her pull him into a hug and even put his arms around her. His mom's familiar scent, both natural and the light perfume in the lotion she favored, enveloped him. There was something else too though, something he'd smelled on other women but never his mom. That was impossible. Wasn't it?

"Where did you go last night?" his mom asked him, stepping out of the hug but keeping her hands on his shoulders.

"Go?"

"Don't play dumb. Cici said you disappeared and didn't come back until this morning."

"I think you know, and unless my nose deceives me, it's better if we avoid the subject for a while; perhaps about nine months?"

"A little less than that."

He could tell she didn't want to smile at him, but the grin refused to say hidden.

"Congratulations, Mom."

"This is so weird! I have a son in college. I was gearing up to be a grandmother and then this happens!"

"How's Dad taking it?"

"Oh, you know," she waved her hand in the air and said in a deeper voice, "What, we're having another kid? Huh."

"Taking it in stride then."

"He did bring me flowers. That's how I knew he knew."

Brayton hadn't seen his mom so happy in months. "Guess you don't know if it's a boy or a girl yet."

She whacked his shoulder. "You know it's way too early for that."

"Um, no. No, I don't. I try not to listen when you and dad…"

"Brayton!"

He laughed. "Don't worry. I've never heard a thing."

Mom sobered and bit her lip. He knew what she was going to say.

"Before you ask Mom, I prefer to finish out the semester here. It's only another week and a half. It's actually safer because I don't have to drive back and forth."

"It's not safer. You're out her all alone. At home you have the entire pack around you. If someone takes you I won't be able to…the stress…" she put her hand on her flat belly.

"Didn't Grandpa tell you?"

"Tell me what?"

He looked around on the very off chance someone was near then leaned forward and whispered, "I'm stronger than he is. I can command witches."

"What? Impossible."

"Nope. Not when you take part in the Luna Initiation ceremony with a Celestial Luna."

"Brayton! You didn't."

"I love her Mom. She's my Luna. I know you think she's the worst thing that ever happened, but she's amazing. She's trying so hard to break the curse once and for all, and she's so close. She only has one more piece to retrieve. I know you're probably worried about the baby, but it will be fine. I'll help her break it before the baby is born."

His mom reached up to touch his cheek. "It's not the baby I'm worried about. It's you."

He felt a sharp pain, then numbness spreading in his cheek. "Mom."

"You left me no choice."

"There's always a choice," he grunted. He willed himself to transform. Nothing.

"What did you do?"

"I am your Luna. She can't have you."

92

"No." He jerked the ring from around his neck and tapped his cheek to break whatever spell his mother had put on him. "She is my Luna. As of now I am no longer part of your pack." Maybe it was overkill but he was tired of fighting. No. He was just plain tired. "Love you Mom. Good luck with the baby."

He transformed and called for Honey to take him.

10

BRAYTON – DECEMBER 10 – WITH HONEY

"*Good morning sleepy head.*"

He'd been awake for a while, just thinking, but now he cracked one eye open to look at the beautiful glowing wolf beside him.

Good morning, irritatingly perky morning person. What time is it? Your glow isn't fooling me. It's still dark."

Honey transformed to give the top of Brayton's head a vigorous rub. "*Time for you to go to school.*"

"*There's no school today. Finals start Thursday.*"

"*Time for you to study then.*"

"*Are you trying to get rid of me?*"

"*No. I just don't want you to fail because of me.*"

"*It won't be because of you.*"

"*What happened? You said something about leaving the pack and then fell asleep.*"

He moved his nose closer so he could rest it on her shoulder. He loved her warm honey smell, even if she could use a bath. "*My mother happened.*"

"*What did she do?*"

"*She poked me with something and I couldn't transform. I used the ring to break the spell, then told her I was no longer part of the pack and called you.*"

"You left your pack because of that?"

"Yep. Oh, and she's expecting."

"Expecting what?"

"A baby."

Honey pulled back and grabbed both sides of his head to look him directly in the eyes. "Really! You're going to be a brother?! Congratulations."

"I had nothing to do with it, but thank you," he said while she kissed his furry cheeks.

"Still, it's good news. Were they trying for another one or is it unplanned."

"I don't know and I don't want to know."

She laughed in his head, then sobered and pinned him with a serious look. "You have to go back. Your mother loves you. She doesn't need to be worrying about you while she's carrying a baby."

"She'll worry no matter where I am or what I'm doing."

"That's not true."

"You think I should let her lock me up? That's what she was planning to do."

"I doubt it. She knows you have finals."

"Honey, she told me that she is my luna and that I can't have you."

"Well, you can't, not yet. Not until I break the curse at least and, you know, people accept me."

"You are already my...wait. I can have you? Like for real have you as my Luna and mate?"

Her eyes grew wide. "No, I mean...I meant..."

No way was he going to let her back out of that statement. "Nope. There's no other meaning for that. I'm going to hold you to it. As soon as we break this curse, you are mine to have and to hold."

"Brayton, I'm not even sixteen."

"For another week. Besides, people used to get married earlier than that."

"And it will take years for people to accept me."

"I've already accepted you and that's all that matters."

"Brayton."

Was he pushing too hard? He prayed he wasn't as he nuzzled her cheek. *"I love you, Honey, with all my heart. I don't care if you're sixteen or sixty, I will always love you."*

"You can't know that. We're basically kids."

"I do know that. It's a wolf thing. Now take us to the nether so I can retrieve my clothes and find all the trackers my mom stuck on me."

"Bossy much?"

"You could always boss me back."

"Will you listen?"

"Do I have a choice?"

She grabbed his ears and put her forehead against his. *"No."*

The dark of the shed faded into the much darker dark of the nether. Brayton transformed and pulled her into a kiss before she could back away, but had she tried to get away? Now he understood why guys gave girls rings. If she accepted a ring, then he'd know for sure how she felt. What if she didn't though? How could he convince her?

Her lips abruptly left his. Before he could complain, she produced a small flashlight and started scanning his clothing while slowly turning him in the odd liquid that was the nether. He felt like a turkey roasting on a spit – a happy, honey-glazed turkey.

Oh no.

He was starting to think like Honey's weird friend. Maybe that was good though. Maybe it would make her like him more.

She plucked something off his backpack and pressed it into his hand. He stabbed the little disk-like object with a claw while she continued her scan.

"All done I think, but you should probably double check when you get back. I'm taking you to the forest by the WOLF field."

He switched back to wolf form so he could talk again. *"I wouldn't call that a forest."*

"Why? There are plenty of trees."

"Let's get something to eat."

"You might have another tracker and I need to breathe."

Brayton did his best begging dog impression.

She rolled her eyes. *"Fine."*

All in all, it was a glorious morning. He convinced her to chase him in her wolf form for a while through the 'forest', although she complained bitterly that her glow was making it impossible for her to sneak up on him. He helpfully pointed out that her big feet and the crunchy leaves were an even bigger give-away. That earned him a much-enjoyed tackle. It wasn't safe for them to go into any restaurants together, but the food she purchased at the gas station wasn't completely horrible, and the long parting kiss afterward was the opposite of horrible. He realized he was still grinning when he arrived at the street where the RV was parked. Rolling his eyes at himself, he consciously made the corners of his mouth go down.

"Hey Brayton."

"Hey Cici." He waved and realized his grin was back. Oh well.

She joined him on the sidewalk. "Where have you been?" She grabbed his shoulder and pulled him toward her to take a sniff. "Oh. Again?"

"Mm-hmm."

"You two are getting pretty serious then?"

"Getting? She's my Luna and someday I hope to make her my wife."

"Did you stay with her all night?"

"Not like you're suggesting, but yeah," he sighed, remembering how nice it was to wake with Honey's warm, furry body next to his, especially in the cold shed.

"What did she say about you being a rogue now?"

"We didn't really talk about it."

"You going to meet up again tonight?"

"I don't know."

"How does she know you want to meet up?"

He abruptly realized what was wrong with Cici's scent and stopped. "Why do you smell so nervous?"

"Brayton, you left the pack."

"Yeah. I think Mom's pregnancy is affecting her brain. She wanted me to go home instead of taking my finals. It was the only thing I could think of to get her off my back."

"Brayton, you are our future alpha. You can't just leave the pack."

He started walking again. His joy from earlier faded into weariness. "I'm tired of fighting her Cici. She's driving me nuts. Besides, I'm sure Dad will take me back in once I explain. I just needed a break."

"Are you sure whatever connection you have with Honey isn't doing something with your mind? The Brayton I know would never leave his pack."

"Honey had nothing to do with it. In fact, she scolded me for leaving."

"What's she doing right now?"

"I don't know."

"Where did you leave her?"

He turned his head to observe Cici's face. "Why are you asking so many questions?"

Cici shook her head. "Your mom's right. Honey's a bad influence on you."

A strong smell of magic wafted from somewhere – maybe behind him? He turned to look, but there was nothing there.

"Sorry Brayton, but it's for your own good."

Cici gave him a strong push from behind. Abruptly he was falling, but the feeling only lasted for a moment before his feet and then his knees landed on something solid.

11

HONEY – DECEMBER 10 – CANADA

Brayton's idea of attaching a find-it compass to an underwater rover and using it to locate the last curse tablet wasn't bad except there weren't many rovers available in the world that could dive as deep as she suspected the tablet was and the few that did exist sounded very expensive to use. What she needed was a retrieve-it spell or maybe...could objects be summoned? Why hadn't she thought of that before?

She pushed away from the computer terminal and took a quick glance around. The library was crowded tonight. She ran her fingers lightly over her mustache to make sure the corners were still glued down, then slung the brown canvas backpack she'd found in a college dumpster over her shoulder.

A petite witch with a pixie cut and leggings that probably did nothing against the winter wind, reached the door to the magical part of the library at the same time she did. Since she was closer to the handle, Honey pulled open the door and gestured for the girl to go ahead of her. The girl scanned Honey from her baggy jeans to her insulated Canadian plaid shirt, up to her new/used brown beanie and smiled. It wasn't just any smile though. It was the kind of smile girls directed at Nathan. Shoot, maybe her disguise was too good. How should she respond? Not like Nathan who could make girls swoon with an eyebrow and definitely not like Luca who would attack them like an eager puppy. The girl giggled and went into the library without Honey doing anything, although the playful look the girl threw over her shoulder when she walked away was concerning.

"Dude, you look like a deer caught in the headlights," a familiar voice said near her ear. "You'll never catch one that way."

"Oh, and you're the expert?" She said over her shoulder.

Her cousin snorted. "Nice 'stash. Follow me. We need to talk."

"How did you know it was me?" Honey asked Michael's back once she was sure no one would hear.

"I sensed your light and your hands are too slim."

"My hands?" She splayed them open in front of her. Her fingers *were* rather long and thin. "That girl didn't seem to mind."

He snorted again. "Her type isn't picky."

The narrow aisle ended in a corner with a round table and another familiar person.

Honey threw in a countrified accent on top of her deepest voice. "Hey Vera."

The young woman looked up and frowned at Honey. "Do I know you?"

Honey grinned and slid into a chair so that her back was to the wall and she could see everyone approaching. "Yep."

"It's Honey," Michael said, sliding into a seat on the Vera's other side.

101

Vera covered her mouth, "Oh, my gosh. I totally didn't recognize you. That beard looks completely real."

"Thanks."

"It looks even better than Michael's."

Michael stroked his barely shadowed jaw. "That's because I just started growing mine out."

"This morning?" Honey asked curiously. Her dad's facial hair would have been twice the length that was on Michael's face after one day.

Vera bust into laughter.

"Very funny. Not all of us can spout hair with a thought," Michael huffed.

"That's true," Honey said, setting her hand on the table behind some books and switching it to a paw and back.

Still chuckling, Vera stretched up and pecked Michael on the cheek. "I like you just the way you are, with or without a beard."

"You two are good then?" Honey asked.

"Yes," Vera replied, putting her hand over Michael's on the table. The fond look Michael was giving Vera was more than enough of a reply on his part.

"Good. I have some news."

"We do too," Vera said.

"You first," Honey nodded, half expecting them to say they'd eloped.

Vera sighed and her shoulders drooped. "I can't do it. I tried and tried, but the maximum I can retrieve something from water is about 300 meters."

That was farther than Honey expected after researching more on water magic. "Oh. That's unfortunate, but I appreciate you trying. Maybe we can come up with something else."

"I need a way to boost my powers," Vera continued. "I'm sure we have something in the bunker, but who knows if it's still there."

"It's not. The place was cleaned out, but I did save your books."

"You did?"

Honey nodded. "Yeah. They were trying to send them all to the library in Boston, but I swiped them back. I don't know where the rest of your things are, but I bet they're in Boston too. There was this witch who said something about preventing dangerous things from getting out in public."

"Those are my things, my family's things!"

"I know. I'll help you get them back if I can," Honey reached over and patted Vera's free hand. "You'll need a safer place to put them though. I put the books in your aunt's workshop and hid the stairs, but they know where everything in the house is now. I wouldn't be surprised if they find the books again."

Vera sighed and looked up at the ceiling. "It's all gone. It's really all gone, everything my family worked for."

Michael put his arm around her. "No it's not. You have more now than your ancestors started with. You have money in the bank. You have property. You have a whole library. I'll help you, and after we're married, I'm sure my family will help you."

"They'll only help if you marry her?" Honey asked, affronted for Vera's sake.

"You don't know much about witch culture, do you?" Michael asked.

"No."

"Witch clans are extremely competitive and they're always trying to bring in more power and knowledge and connections. Marrying Vera will be seen as a boon to my family because she has such an ancient lineage."

"You mean they'll try to take her stuff for themselves?"

"No, but they'll expect access, especially since no other families have had access to the Lambert collection for generations."

"Yeah, thanks to my aunt," Vera mumbled, dipping her face. A single tear trailed down her cheek.

Honey started to commiserate over the unfairness of it all then realized how hypocritical that would be since she'd already started using Vera's library. "Access isn't so bad when you think about it, especially if you can wield it to get the things you need. Maybe you could put a spell in place to ensure only the people you want to have access can get to it."

"I need a place to put a spell on first. I can't go back to that house. Every time I'll go in the library I'll be imagining my mom stuck in the wall and I…"

Michael pulled a sobbing Vera against his shoulder and sent Honey a cold glare.

"Well, um I know where there's a pirate ship and since you're a water witch, maybe you could live there for now." Honey threw out. "I don't know if it floats though. There are cannon holes."

Vera lifted her head off Michael's shoulder and swiped the tears off her cheeks with a loud sniff. "Yes. That would be perfect. I can seal the holes until they're properly fixed."

"Do you know how to operate a sailing ship?" Michael asked dubiously.

"No, but I can learn. There's a book on sailing in my library."

"By yourself?"

"I come from a long line of sailors."

"Maybe you can park it like a houseboat," Honey suggested, silently agreeing with Michael about Vera's sailing skills, "Until you find something more permanent."

"I like that idea even better."

"There's also an abandoned farmhouse not far from here. You could buy it and fix it up or find another one like it." Honey added.

Vera shivered. "It's too cold here."

"Where does one park a houseboat?" Michael asked, squeezing Vera's shoulders with the arm he still had draped around them. "I think it would be fun to live in a pirate ship for a while."

"Florida, Texas, North Carolina, there are lots of places," Vera shrugged.

"Just let me know where you want it," Honey said, "and I'll deliver."

"That was epic, by the way," Michael grinned across the table. "One of my uncles was there. He said the ones in charge were all excited because they could feel something big coming, then all of a sudden, something *really* big came. He said it was like fishing for a minnow and catching a whale.

He's not a Wixx, so he wasn't hanging out with the Wixx witches, but Madame Wixx was there and my uncle swears she smiled after you disappeared again."

His uncle had to be mistaken about the smile unless her great-grandmother was planning something else. Great. Yet another thing to worry about.

"Was my grandmother there? Where was that anyway?"

"Yes and somewhere in Kentucky."

"So why are you here?" Michael asked. "I assume you didn't dress up like that for fun."

"Never assume, but I had another idea. Maybe you'll know the answer. Can *things* be summoned?"

"Things?"

"Yeah, like, say a cursed tablet instead of me."

Michael rubbed the fuzz on his chin. "Oh, I see where you're going with this."

Vera shook her head. "I doubt it. Can you imagine if a robber figured out how to do it? Nothing would be safe."

"If it works the same way, summoning a thing would require a related item or something that was previously a part of it, which most things don't have, plus there are spells to prevent summoning."

"Are you using one?" Michael asked.

"I am now."

"I'm sure there's a book on summoning in the library... here." Vera sighed.

"I'll go ask," Michael volunteered.

Honey reached out and grabbed his arm before he could get away. "It's not that I don't trust you, but you're not going to turn me in, are you?"

"No. I promise. I'm on your side. Besides, nobody would believe me right now anyway, Butch."

"Butch?"

"I gotta call you something, eh?"

"Not Butch," she whisper-shouted as he walked away.

Turned out there *was* such a thing as a summoning spell for things, but to reach especially long distances such as to the middle of the ocean, you needed lots of witches.

"Unless we take a boat out to the spot, then you only have to summon it a few miles," Vera said.

"Through water," Honey pointed out.

"Shouldn't be a problem. Not with me there," Vera proclaimed confidently.

"There are a lot of shipping boats that cross the Atlantic," Michael said, showing Vera and Honey his phone screen. "We could sneak onto one of those."

"We?"

"Of course. I'll bring some friends too," Michael grinned.

"No. There are very few people I can trust."

"I won't tell them where we're going and I'll make sure they are pro-Honey."

"People lie. Please Michael, don't tell anyone. I'll find some people."

"What if I say that my fiance'," he and Vera exchanged smiles, "wants to see how many people it takes to retrieve something from the bottom of the ocean? You can come like you are now. No one will recognize you. Everyone will think it's just another college adventure. We could do it at the full moon!"

"That's Sunday, right? It will probably take me longer than that to find the right ship and then it probably takes a while to get to the destination."

"Right after finals then or during Winter break."

It was a crazy idea, but, assuming she could find a large, flat space on a ship where no one could see them, it was the best idea so far. "All right, it's a possibility. I need to do some research and figure out what port to go to and what ship to target and check out their security. I'll let you know. Don't say anything to anyone until I'm sure it's doable though."

Michael waved his phone at her. "We should exchange numbers."

"I don't have a phone, but I'll take your number."

After researching online Honey concluded the smartest way to get to Boston to check out the docks would be by car (too bad she didn't have one) or motorcycle (if only it were warmer) and would take at least 12 hours and would cost roughly $100 in gas. Brayton would probably take her, but she'd have to wait until after finals and she was certain someone would notice if he suddenly took off on a road trip. On the other hand, using her anchor on the floor of the warehouse in Boston would be nearly instantaneous and free, as long as she didn't get caught.

It was risky, extremely risky, but surely the warehouse wasn't busy all night, every night. If she got there in the wee hours of the morning, say 3 am, it should be a dark, empty building with a few guards, right? If her wolf form didn't glow, she might be able to pass herself off as a stray dog that got in somehow. How could she hide the glow? Curious, she googled dog leotards thinking she could wear a black one, then nearly laughed out loud at the images that popped up. The lab in the black wasn't bad, but the little dogs with skinny legs squeezed into tight blue and red onesies with their big white fluffy heads poking out the tops were ridiculous. The hoodies for dogs looked much more doable, except her glowing rear would still be exposed. Pants. She needed pants.

On her way to the thrift store to find sweats that would fit her wolf, she spotted an even better, cheaper costume, maybe. She looked around carefully, then sent the wolf-sized box to the nether. It wouldn't hurt to have options.

A couple of hours and a nice dinner later, she was ready.

"Brayton, are you there?"

She settled herself in the boiler room while she waited for a response. It was earlier than she normally talked to him. He was probably busy.

"I guess you're studying. You better be studying. I'm going to bed early. I've got plans for tonight. I think I've found a way to get the last curse, it will take some scouting though. I'll talk to you tomorrow. Goodnight."

12

BRAYTON – DECEMBER 11 – LOCATION UNKNOWN

Loud clanging startled him awake, surprising him not just because it was unexpected, but because he'd managed to fall asleep on the cold cement.

"Rise and shine nephew of mine!"

"Uncle Rick?"

He couldn't remember the last time he'd seen his uncle. He was always away on a mission somewhere although Brayton couldn't say for whom. Even that was top secret. He looked like Brayton remembered except for the scraggly beard.

"Got it first try." His uncle tugged at his beard, "Guess I need to work on my disguise."

"What are you doing here and where is here?"

"Like it?" his uncle said, waving his hand at the narrow stairs and the cement walls outside of the metal cage Brayton was trapped in.

"Not really."

His uncle shrugged. "It's my buddy's emergency shelter. He's out of town for a couple of months. I didn't figure he would mind if I borrowed it for a bit."

"Why are we here?"

"Your mother was worried about you and she asked for my help."

"I have finals tomorrow. I need to study."

"Don't worry about them. Your mom's taking care of it. She said something about withdrawing due to mental issues from the torture you experienced."

"I am not suffering from mental issues."

"It's nothing to be ashamed of. A lot of my buddies suffer from PTSD."

"I am not suffering from PTSD. If anyone is, it's Mom. Will you please let me out of here?"

"No can do, little buddy. Now why don't you tell me about this girl of yours. I hear she's quite pretty."

He didn't want to use his power on a family member but he didn't want to have to repeat his classes either. "Let. Me. Out."

His uncle shook his head and jangled the dog tags around his neck. "It's not going to work. I had these charmed a long time ago, plus the cage inhibits the powers of anyone inside."

Brayton had figured that out yesterday after trying unsuccessfully all day to transform. He didn't know his uncle very well, but his uncle wasn't a pregnant 44-year-old woman. Maybe Brayton could make him see reason. "What did Mom tell you? I think you're missing some key details."

"All right, tell me your side of the story."

13

HONEY – DECEMBER 12 – BOSTON

Honey peaked out from under the edge of the cardboard. Except for the lights from the emergency exits and the faint glow of the numbers reading 2:50 am on her watch, everything in the warehouse was dark. That was good. It didn't mean there weren't cameras around though, or magical detectors. Surprisingly, even with her magical sight, the only wards she could see were at the edges of the doors. With the box still on her back, she slowly crawled to the deeper shadows in front of the loading deck edge. From there she just had to work her way around the room to one of the large entrance doors, take down one of the wards, and she'd be free.

Something whined right in front of her face. Honey froze. Was that what she thought it was?

"*You?*" she whispered in her mind.

The magic dog whined again, but with a happy note, and rubbed his head against hers.

Making sure she was completely in shadow, she transformed so she could rub between his ears. "What are you doing here?"

He pressed eagerly into her hand, making her chuckle.

"You want to go with me on an adventure?"

He barked and wagged his tail and then lunged with his sharp little teeth.

"No! I'm in the middle of something. I can't…" Too late.

A familiar greenspace replaced the dark of the warehouse. A moment later, an equally familiar stern-faced witch marched out of a copse of trees.

"Luna," the witch spin out.

"Mother Lambert."

"Where is mine descendent?"

"Safe. Engaged."

"To that man?"

"Yes."

The witch raised her hand. "Thou should hast done as I asked"

Honey thickened her shield. "The world is not like it was when you were alive. Marriages aren't arranged. Vera needed to make the decision herself and to make it official, they have to get married by someone who's licensed, which isn't me."

The witches hand started glowing. "Still, Thou should hast done as I asked."

"You're going to kill me? Do you know where you are?"

"Doth thou?" the woman challenged.

"I do. You're in the Boston library somewhere. The house in Texas is in shambles. All of your family's artifacts were boxed up and carted here. I'm not sure if Vera will be able to get them back."

"What about the books and our grimoires?"

"They were here, but I took them back to the house. I don't know if they've found them again yet."

"*Thou* took them?"

113

"Yes. It wasn't fair what happened to Vera and I count her as a friend."

Mother Lambert dropped her hand. "What of the curse?"

"I'm still working on retrieving the last piece, but I think I've figured out a way."

"Where is it?"

"The bottom of the ocean."

"What is thy plan?"

"Take a boat until we get close, then use a summoning spell."

The woman nodded thoughtfully. "Thou shalt want many witches to counter the anti-magic effect of water."

"How many?"

"It depends on the depth. Water witches would be best, but lacking that, at least ten."

Ten. She hoped Michael had a lot of friends.

"Or," the woman said, placing her hand on top of her spell-dog's head, "mine guardian can retrieve it."

"He can do that?"

"Yes."

"What do you want in return?" because there was no way this woman didn't want something.

"I want thou to take mine necklace and all our other artifacts to Vera."

"I don't know where she's staying and your school isn't safe but... I know at least one place I might be able to stash your things temporarily. I think it's part of a wolf's territory. Let me ask the alpha if it would be okay."

Mother Lambert was already shaking her head. "That's unacceptable."

"It's an abandoned house in the middle of farmland. If it *is* in wolf territory, other witches will hesitate to bother your things," Honey argued. "He's a nice man and he's sworn an oath to help me."

The woman's head-shaking paused. "He is sworn to thee?"

"Yes, and I helped him avoid a battle."

"He owes thou."

Honey shrugged. "Since the battle was over me, I think we're even, but he is not against me and he has a kind heart."

"Thou will contact him."

"I'll do it right now," Honey agreed, then remembered what time it was. "Actually, I better wait until morning, but I could store your things in the nether until I ask Vera where she wants them."

Mother Lambert nodded. "That is acceptable. Once she receives the items, I shall send mine guardian to retrieve the tablet."

"Can he deliver it to me or will I need to come here?"

"You will need to come here."

Honey nodded, the guardian spell probably didn't include delivery service.

"Quickly then." The woman waved her hand.

"Wait!"

Too late. Honey found herself standing in a room with a long counter, shelves full of boxes and artifacts and corners full of cameras. Phooey.

She dropped to the floor and pushed her back up against the counter. The room was almost completely dark so maybe no one had seen? She wasn't sure how magical cameras

115

worked and they had to be magical with all the magic in the room.

"There are cameras," she whispered at the inquisitive whine near her ear. She could destroy them or make them disappear, or perhaps easiest and least damaging, just cover them, but if anyone was watching, they'd notice something was wrong.

"Which stuff is Vera's?" There was no way everything in the room had come out of her house.

The Guardian disappeared. A moment later, something fell on her head.

"An inventory," Honey whispered after she'd recovered from her near heart attack and had deciphered some of the writing in the slim notebook by using the faint glow from her wolf paw to light the page. Eleven boxes and the items in each were listed, some with check-marks beside them and some with small lines of different lengths next to them.

"Do you know where the boxes are?"

The guardian gave a little whine. Did that mean he didn't know or had they been unpacked?

"Can you show me where the sun pendant is, where Mother Lambert is?"

The guardian looked up at the counter, then back at her.

"Great. Are all her things still in this room at least?"

Another whine.

"Can you show me where the other things are? Not yet," she said when he started for the door.

How was she going to do this without getting caught? It would have been a lot easier to go with her original plan and find a ship to the middle of the ocean.

"Okay, here's the plan. I'll read the items on the list and if they're in this room, can you stand next to them or indicate where they are? I need an idea of where everything is."

She put her finger under the first item to read it. The little lines on the side suddenly got big enough to read.

Iron fleam. Likely pre-1500's. Magic level 1. Cleansing spell.

What was a fleam?

The second item said, *Top hat. 18th century. Magic level 3. Purpose unknown. Further study recommended.*

Why would someone spell a hat? Was it to make them smarter or perhaps so they wouldn't lose it? She'd have to sniff that one. How would whoever had written this rate the medallion? She skimmed down the list to the last checked item.

Solar medallion. Magic level 10+. Dangerous. Further study requir____.

The pen mark disappeared off the edge of the page.

Honey looked up into the guardian's faintly glowing eyes. "What did you do? Did you bite him or her?"

The guardian cocked its head.

"Did you just scare them?"

Its head tilted farther.

"Okay, I'm guessing that means boxes 6 through 11 are untouched? Is that them?" She pointed to the two stacks at the end of the shelves in front of her with glowing numbers on the sides.

Her friend barked and wagged its transparent tail.

"Here goes nothing."

She sped herself up and zipped to squat in between the shelves where she could easily reach the boxes. To be sure they weren't empty, she tilted the lid open on the top one and looked inside. Something was in there, but everything was wrapped in brown paper.

"Guess I'll have to check later. I can always return it." Wouldn't that surprise someone?

She touched the bottom box with the back of her wrist to send the whole stack to the nether. The notebook she was holding started flashing. '*Box removed without clearance*' was scrolling in bright red over all the lines belonging to the missing boxes. She quickly brought the boxes back.

"Phooey. Should have known it wouldn't be that easy."

She needed something to put the stuff in, like that old box she'd found, or a bag.

All her bags were full.

The tents were mostly empty though.

She pulled Jay's tent into the space between the shelves where the cameras couldn't see and started transferring things one box at a time. When that was done, she went down each aisle with the guardian and stuffed everything it pointed out into a pair of Jay's pants with the legs tied shut. Whoever had made the labels had helpfully put 'LBC', she assumed to note they were from the Lambert Collection.

Finally, all that was left were the items on the counter, which looked to be about one box worth.

"Take out the cameras or super speed? What do you think?" she asked her partner-in-crime.

He wagged his tail.

"You are so helpful. A combination it is."

She shot magical shields at the cameras to interfere with whatever connection they had before rushing forward and replacing the partially emptied box on the counter with a completely empty one, then removed the shields. If anyone was watching, they'd hopefully think it was just a blip, assuming magical cameras did that. After emptying out the box, she blocked the camera several more times, working her way down the counter and taking and replacing Vera's things with items from the shelves. She was nearly done when light abruptly appeared through the cracks around the door. She scurried back between the shelves and sent the tent and her pants-bag to the nether.

A key scraped in the lock. Uh-oh. She looked around for a place to hide. The shelves were too full for her to climb on or up and the cameras in the back corners would catch her if she went behind the shelves. She'd just have to play it by ear. She squatted so she could see the door from the shelves but her eyes wouldn't be at eye-level.

The person who entered wasn't the middle-aged, beer-bellied guard that Honey had envisioned. *She* was wearing a guard uniform consisting of a jacket with a patch on the shoulder, Honey had gotten that right, but the young woman was fit and walked with a military bearing. Even her hair, which she had pulled back into a tight bun, gave off a military vibe. For a moment, Honey missed her own hair, but it would have never cooperated like that.

It was a good thing her eyes had already started to adjust to the light in the hallway behind the woman else Honey would have been blinded when the guard flipped on the light. She had a good view through a crack between the boxes and the end of the shelf and she knew the top of her head couldn't be seen but Honey still had to force herself not to duck when the woman's eyes swept over the room.

"The life sensor's not picking up anything," the woman spoke into her collar, "but there's a lot of magical interference in here."

Life sensor? That must be that small neon-light bulb-looking thing the guard was waving slowly in front of her. Would it be able to detect her through her shields? Should she disable it?

Faintly, Honey heard the voice in the woman's earplug say something that sounded like "Proceed with caution."

The woman took a careful step into the room, still waving her life sensor. Honey thickened her shields. The sensor started to beep and glow a faint green.

The woman stopped. "There's something in here."

Honey quickly dismantled the protection charms she sensed on the woman and froze her.

"Secure the door and wait for backup," came clearly through the comm.

Time was up. Honey zapped the cameras and quickly scooped the remaining items on the counter into the box she'd brought as a disguise. She was very careful to use a pen to move the sun pendant.

There were probably cameras in the hallway, but she couldn't leave, not yet. She hadn't found the top hat and she was certain Mother Lambert wouldn't carry through on her part of the deal unless Honey returned everything. She sent the box to the nether, then transformed into her hoodie-covered wolf self, complete with long black shorts to hide her tail and black socks to hide her paws. The only glowing thing visible was her face if she looked up.

"Lead me to the rest of the items," she whispered to her companion who was now standing next to her looking over her strange attire with a mixture of curiosity and amusement, or so she imagined.

"Go. Fast. I'll catch up."

With a little bark, the guardian shot off into the hallway to the right. She gave him a moment, then sped up her molecules and zipped down the hallway herself. She didn't bother to test the doorknob where he stopped. She made it vanish and reappear after she'd opened the door, then slipped in and pulled the door shut, plunging herself into darkness once again.

The security the dark offered was deceptive. There were even more cameras in this room and no shelves to hide between. It was all tables. She followed her companion beneath the tables to the far corner where the elusive top hat sat proudly near the edge of the table. Honey transformed under the table so she could grab it along with the pair of earrings the guardian indicated.

Rapid footsteps belonging to multiple sets of feet thundered down the hall. The light shining through the half-glass door dimmed and the doorknob rattled.

"It's locked. Are you sure you saw something here?" A muffled male voice asked.

A flashlight beam hit the wall by her head and slowly moved to the left.

"How many more items are left?" she whispered.

The guardian gave a little whine.

"Are there more items left?"

Another whine.

"I assume that means yes." She wished she hadn't left the list in the other room so she could get an idea of how many things she still needed to retrieve. A sudden thought struck her. "Can't you get them and send them to the pendant? Now that I have the pendant, Mother Lambert will be able to give everything to Vera."

Her friend wagged his tail in excitement with her for a moment, then slumped with another whine.

"What? Can't you do it?"

His whine sounded distinctly like a no this time.

"Mother Lambert *lied* to me? Are you telling me you *can't* retrieve things?"

The magical creature looked sorrowfully up to her with the best sad puppy-dog look she'd ever witnessed.

"Please tell me she didn't lie and that I'm not risking everything for nothing."

Her friend ducked his head even more.

Mother Lambert had only wanted to use her. Nothing new there. At least she had some leverage. She was the only person who could pull Vera's thing back out of the nether after all.

The light disappeared and so did the shape at the door after one more attempt at the knob.

"They'll be watching the hallway now. How are we going to get out of here? Maybe I should go and try again tomorrow."

Her companion groaned.

"Not a fan? I guess we do have an advantage right now since they don't know what I'm looking for. Also, I can go through walls and ceilings. Did I mention that?"

The guardian gave a surprised little squeak.

"Are we on the right floor or do we need to go up or down?"

The guardian glowed at her blankly.

"Can you point your nose in the direction I need to go."

The spell obediently did a classic pointer pose directly at the door.

"Across the hall?"

The guardian didn't move.

"I might be able to handle that. Is that the last place?"

It still didn't move. She would have thought it was frozen except she knew she hadn't used any magic. She reached up and stroked its transparent head. "You can stop pointing now."

The spell relaxed and pressed happily into her hand.

"Silly."

She could still hear voices in the hallway. No doubt they were trying to figure out if anything was missing in the other room. How long would it take them to find the list of items she'd tucked into the side of one of the now-empty boxes? She peered up from under her table to the drop ceiling. She could go up to the next floor and across, but what room would she end up in and under what furniture, if any. No, it was probably better if she used the door and just went fast.

Keeping to the darkest shadows and the center of the tables, she crawled toward the front of the room.

"Can you see how many people are in the hallway and if they're looking this way?"

The guardian vanished. A few moments later he reappeared by her side and gave three quick yips.

"Three. Is anyone looking this way?"

Her companion growled.

How was she going to do this?

"Is that the last item? Growl if it's not."

The guardian whined.

What was she afraid of? People wanted to kill her for being a hybrid, but the guards wouldn't know who she was. They'd likely try to trap her with magic and fail. She was innocent of all the crimes they'd accused her of so far though. If they caught her on camera and figured out who she was, she'd be branded as a thief, and those few people who were for her might turn against her too.

"We're going in another way."

She pictured what she wanted and tapped on the floor. A square hole with tapered edges big enough for her to crawl through appeared in front of her. She stuck a glowing paw in and inspected the space. Whoever had hung the drop ceiling had kindly dropped it low enough that there was plenty of space to crawl between the floor and the ceiling. She carefully slipped into the hole so that she was on her back, praying the whole time that the flimsy metal grid holding the ceiling tiles could hold her. Once she was all the way through, she made another, smaller tapered hole, then put her hand up through it to put the large square back. The dark after she plugged the little hole was almost absolute.

"I guess we could hang out here for a while."

The guardian growled in her ear.

"Kidding."

Keeping her hands and feet on the rails that held up the tiles, she crab-walked the five or so feet to where she knew the door was above them. She expected to run into a support beam, but instead her head hit a solid cinder block wall. Excellent. She wouldn't have to worry about messing up the integrity of the building. She tapped a Honey-sized hole into the wall and crawled through, then tapped the wall piece back. It was backwards, but no one would notice until they replaced the ceiling tiles. Interestingly, the magic level was noticeably stronger on this side of the wall, much stronger and more evil-feeling and familiar.

"It's a grimoire isn't it?"

The guardian huffed in her ear.

"Philomena's grimoire?"

The spell whined.

"You're making me risk everything to get that women's horrible spell?"

This time it growled. That was a no, she was pretty sure.

She pulled her backpack from the nether and found the new stash ring she'd been working on. "Better hope this works."

The room smelled just as evil as it had the first time. Still on her back, Honey peered around the room through the hole she'd made in the floor but didn't see any cameras or other magic waiting to pounce. Surely they'd added some new security features since her last visit. After sending the laser grid over the floor to the nether with her ring, she took off her beanie and tossed it into the air. Another magical scent she couldn't pick out over the other smells joined the rest but her hat just flopped on the ground.

"At least it's not more lasers."

She recognized the spell as soon as her shoulders were above the floor.

"Freeze charms." She layered her shield so the charms would only affect the outermost layer and climbed the rest of the way inside. Staying low, she retrieved her beanie and sent it to the nether. She didn't really need it with her hoodie and full-coverage face shield she never thought she'd wear again.

"Where is it?" she whispered to the spell dog now riding on her shoulder in mini form.

It ran down her arm toward a large book open on top of a sturdy-looking desk. A partially filled notebook sat next to it.

"Looks like they were translating it."

Her companion growled.

"I agree. Completely rude. They didn't get far though."

The hair on the back of her neck tingled. She turned and ducked just in time to avoid the shoe-sized object flying at her face. The object flew over her head and over the desk. A moment later, everything exploded. The desk and the book flew at her at the same time the floor beneath her gave way. On reflex, she sped up her molecules, grabbed hold of the corner of the book, and sent herself to the nether.

14

BRAYTON – DECEMBER 12 – LOCATION UNKNOWN

"She beat up some homeless humans in Australia?"

"It was like ten-to-one."

"She used her magic?"

Brayton frowned at his uncle's question. They'd been over this. "No. She didn't need to. She's good and they were just humans,"

"How did she get away?"

"The video shows her running."

"To where? Did she portal?"

"I don't know. She doesn't tell me where she goes."

"Think she went to that cave?"

Brayton shrugged. "She could have."

"Does she still go there?"

"I don't know. She goes to lots of places."

"How?"

"With her magic."

"Does it work like a portal?"

"No. It's more instantaneous and you don't feel bad afterward. You just can't breath."

"Can't breath?"

"She always tells me to hold my breath. We travel through water I think."

His uncle's eyebrows went up half-way to his hairline. "Water?"

"It feels like water."

Brayton grinned to himself remembering the way Honey had turned him the last time they were in the nether.

"Does she stay there? Is that why no one can find her?" his uncle asked.

"You can't breathe there."

"Are you wet afterward?"

"No."

"How does she pick a place to go?"

"She finds places no one else is."

"How?"

That was a stupid question. "The same way you would. She looks."

"She can see ahead before she travels?"

"No, of course not. She…" wait a second, why was he telling his uncle, his mother's brother, how Honey traveled?

"…she plants…" he squeezed his babbling lips together with his own fingers.

"Yes?" his uncle asked, leaning forward slightly.

Brayton fought his mouth, but something had control. If he could just change the word. Not seeds - trees. Yes! She'd planted a tree. He kept that firmly in his mind as his fingers released his lips. "Tree!"

"What?"

"She planted a tree."

"Yeah," Brayton agreed. He couldn't remember ever spending this much time with his mom's brother. He was surprisingly easy to talk to.

"Do you know where she is now?"

"No."

"Didn't you just see her last night?"

"Yeah, but again, she never tells me where she's going or when she's coming. She's afraid someone will try to force the information from me."

"She's more concerned about her safety than yours?"

"No! She's trying to keep a target off my back."

"Doesn't seem to be working. How many times have you been tortured to near death? If you knew where she was, you could tell them and you'd be fine."

"First of all, Honey is my Luna. I would die before I willingly betrayed her. Second, the one time I did tell someone where she was, unwillingly I might add, the guy tried to kill me anyway."

"Mmm. Where did you guys go on your date last night?"

Did it count as a date? "We didn't go anywhere. I fell asleep."

His uncle snorted. "You had your lovely Luna all to yourself and fell asleep?"

He shrugged. "It was a long day."

"You went somewhere. Your mom said you disappeared into thin air. Where did you go?"

"A shed."

"What shed?"

Oh shoot. Had he said that? He needed to be more careful. "One of many," he mumbled, thinking of all the sheds around the pack's land.

"I heard she has a lot of friends," his uncle commented, leaning casually back on the steps and looking up at the dark sky through the open door.

"She is very good at making friends," Brayton agreed, "because she's a nice person."

"I heard she made friends with a portal witch."

"I think everyone's heard that."

"Do they hang out?"

"I doubt it. Frederica goes to a witch school and everyone there probably knows about Honey."

His uncle didn't move, but something about his posture caught Brayton's attention.

"How do they know her?"

"Honey rescued her. It was all over the news."

"How does she know the girl though?"

"I'm not sure exactly. Honey did mention she worked up there in the spring."

"She had a job?"

"Yeah, I mentioned that already didn't I? That guy who burned me kidnapped her and she escaped to Canada."

"Oh, that's right. Where in Canada again?"

"I don't know," Brayton said truthfully.

His uncle sat up, shaking his head. "She really doesn't tell you much, does she?"

"No. I told you, she's smart. I mean, if you were using that spell that makes a person talk, you'd know everything now."

"Indeed."

Wait a second. Why was he spilling so much to his uncle, a veritable stranger? Was his *uncle* using a spell on him?

Brayton blinked twice and slowly scanned the bars of the cage. They were glowing just like they were the first time he looked, but now that he looked closer, he could see different colors weaving together.

"Brayton, you all right?"

"Not really, no," he said, focusing on the awful man in front of him. "You've been playing me the whole time."

"What do you mean?"

"I've had a truth spell used on me before. You've mixed it with a spell to lower inhibitions or something. You used magic on me, a wolf. Here I thought you stood for good. Hypocrite."

"Said the pot."

"I haven't used magic on anyone."

"No, I don't suppose you have." His uncle stood and checked his watch. "Well, it's been nice chatting. Sorry I have to leave for a while. Here are a couple of MREs and some water. I'll be back tonight."

"What time is it?"

"About 5 am."

"You're just going to leave me here?"

"Not forever, just until I can get that little witch's claws out of your head. Lucky for me, you left your pack, rogue. No one will be able to find you here. The whole place is warded."

"Better a rogue than a hypocritical, lying, prejudiced idiot."

His uncle didn't bother responding before stomping up the stairs and leaving Brayton in near total darkness.

15

HONEY – DECEMBER 12 – PENDANT

"Thee got it."

"Yes," Honey said, tearing off her face shield. It was covered in dust and bits of desk. The book she was still holding; however, looked pristine.

"And I didst not forswear," Mother Lambert sniffed above her. "The guardian couldn't get into that room and 'twere easier to hast thou collect all the other items. Pulling things into the pendant doth take much magical energy and I didn't wisheth to run low."

"How do you obtain magical energy?" Honey asked curiously.

"The pendant absorbs it from the air and from visitors. Not too much," she added at Honey's frown.

"You were in a magical library. You can't be in a much more magical environment than that."

"Aye, and the visitors hast been plentiful of late."

"That's a grimoire," another voice said behind Honey.

Honey nearly turned, but then thought better of it and pulled her hood down a little more.

"The Lambert grimoire, which should'st ne'r hast been taken from the Lambert premises," Mother Lambert said regally.

"It was abandoned."

"No," Honey said picking herself up from the ground where she'd landed after the guardian spell had bit her, again. "The owner was in shock and only left to compose herself. She didn't realize the other witches would swoop in like a flock of hungry vultures."

"Who are you?" the older witch behind Honey demanded.

"Who are you?"

"Agatha Snelling, DM, Assistant Curator of magical artifacts for the National Library of Witchcraft and Wizardry."

"I thought people didn't use the term wizard anymore," Honey said.

"It's historic!"

"What is she doing here?" Honey asked Mother Lambert

"She poked the pendant," the spell woman said with a smirk.

"I did not."

The woman's voice had moved closer. Honey broke through the protection spells she sensed and froze the woman before finally turning to take a look. She was older, in her fifties perhaps, and filled out as women that age tended to be, but not fat. Her dark pink jacket, matching skirt, and sensible heels looked very professional except for being rumpled.

"How long has she been here?"

"Too longeth," Mother Lambert groused.

"Why didn't you return her?"

"She wouldn't concur to return the artifacts to mine descendant and she's cursed to stay."

"Can't you overrule the curse?"

"I didst not set it."

133

Honey sighed. She was starting to feel a little shaky from using so much magic and from nearly being killed, but she couldn't leave the woman here. She looked over the woman with her magic sight. The curse had manifested itself as a green chain around the woman's ankle that slithered off somewhere into the forest. Honey easily sliced through it with a claw.

"She's curse free. Can you send her back now?"

Mother Lambert shook her head. "I can only sendeth her directly outside the pendant."

"I'll take her back, then I need to find some food and rest for a while. I'll get you to Vera as soon as I can."

"Thee should'st come back here."

"I have to find Vera."

"Thee were almost killed by a grenade. Tis safe here."

"You know about grenades?"

The woman gestured to her guardian. "I hast seen and learned many things through the eyes of mine guardian and from my mine descendants."

Honey rubbed her forehead. "I don't understand where it came from. There was no one else there and the witches wouldn't be so foolish as to set one off in their library."

"Indeed. Can thee not bethink of a spell that wouldst allow one to sendeth a grenade directly to thee?"

"A seeking spell," Honey raised her wrist, "but I made protections against it."

"It is difficult to block one's own blood."

"But no one has my blood."

"Art thee sure?"

Honey sighed. She wasn't. Who knew how many people had helped themselves to that vial before it was destroyed.

"What has happened to the library?" the thawing woman demanded.

Honey ducked her head beneath her hood and froze the woman's legs so she couldn't move but decided to answer. The woman would find out eventually. Better she learned what really happened from Honey than the lies and speculation she'd get from everyone else. "Someone sent a grenade to the restricted room. I barely escaped."

"And what were you doing in the restricted room?" the woman huffed.

"Retrieving a stolen item," Honey said. "Believe me, I did not enjoy my time there." She shivered.

"Stealing more like. That grimoire is dangerous and belongs to the library. You can't…"

Honey froze the rest of the woman. "I'll take her back now."

"Thee shall cometh back?"

"I plan to."

"I'll send mine guardian with thee."

Honey squatted and grabbed hold of the frozen woman's leg, then sent herself and the woman back to the library loading dock.

16

BRAYTON – DECEMBER 12 – LOCATION UNKNOWN

Brayton jerked awake, then winced at the bright light shining squarely in his eyes. Footsteps pounded on the narrow stairs and mercifully, the bright light vanished.

"Brayon, why did Honey bomb the National Witch Library in Boston?" his uncle demanded.

Brayton lay his head back on the hard, cold cement. He didn't know if it was the MRE he'd eaten or something else, but his stomach did not feel good. No, his whole body did not feel good. "What are you talking about?"

"Someone bombed the National Witch Library."

"Okay."

"Did Honey do it?"

"How would I know?" Brayton grouched, then winced. His head hurt too, probably from trying to force his stupid non-laser eye to work.

"She didn't mention any plans?"

"Honey would never blow up a library. She likes them too much."

"Her magical signature was all over the bomb blast."

"She doesn't know how to make bombs," Brayton insisted, even as his stomach dropped somewhere, maybe into the cement.

136

"You said she was a chemistry major."

"So? Did you know how to make bombs after two semesters of basic chemistry?"

"Yes, actually."

"Goodie for you. I guarantee Honey didn't do it. She'd never be so stupid as to leave her signature everywhere. And, if she did blow up the library, it was for a very good reason."

There was a long pause. Brayton could hear his uncle doing something but he didn't bother to open his eyes. Even the dim bulb overhead was irritating. His headache got suddenly worse. It felt like a vise was squeezing his head.

"Brayton, think back, did Honey ever mention Boston?"

"Boston? Why would she go to Boston?" Really, why did she go to anywhere? Where was she now?

The vise squeezed harder. Shoot. He turned just in time to spew the MRE to the side instead of up in the air. Not unsurprisingly, it looked even grosser than it had before he ate it. He did feel better though. Even the vice around his head had loosened.

"You okay?" His uncle almost sounded concerned.

Brayton sat up, mostly to get away from the smell, and wiped his mouth with the back of his hand. "Yeah. I don't think that MRE agreed with me."

"You said Honey was working on finding a way to pull something up from the bottom of the ocean."

He'd said that? Why would he say that?

"Did she find it?"

"I don't know."

"She hasn't contacted you?"

"How could she contact me? I'm trapped in a cage."

"But you said she could do telepathy now."

He had?

The vise tightened around his head again. He managed to almost hit the pile of vile as his stomach emptied itself a second time. This time it didn't do anything to relieve the pain.

"Has she contacted you?" his uncle demanded.

Brayton puked a third time, but there wasn't much left.

"Dammit, answer me."

"NO!" Brayton yelled.

The squeezing feeling abruptly ceased. "See, that wasn't so hard."

For the first time Brayton noticed his uncle was holding a device like a TV remote but with three dials. His own uncle was torturing him now? Did Mom know?

"I'll get you something to clean up that mess," his uncle said, jogging back up the stairs.

17

BRAYTON – DECEMBER 14 – LOCATION UNKNOWN

Moist, fresh air poured down the steps. Since no light blinded him, it must be night again. How many days had it been...three, four? His fuzzy brain had lost track.

"Brayton, you awake?"

He didn't bother to respond. It wouldn't matter if he wasn't. The A-hat would turn on his brain squeezer and make him puke again. The joke was on him. There wasn't anything left to puke up.

"Brayton?"

The A-hat actually sounded a little worried. Good.

"Brayton, answer me."

The magic in the bars pressed against him, urging him to answer, but each time it affected him less. Too bad the damage had already been done. Had Honey realized he'd blabbed all her secrets? Is that why she wasn't speaking to him or was the magic in the bars preventing it? The only other possibility was the one he didn't dare think about too much – that she was dead. The fuzz in his head doubled.

"Brayton! Damn your stubborn hide, you need to eat."

His stomach gurgled at the lovely scent of fried potatoes and greasy beef. He could picture the bag he heard crinkling in his jailer's hand, but he wouldn't let it affect him. He'd learned his lesson. He doubted his uncle had meant to poison him, but he'd slipped something in his food. He'd be a fool to accept anything from him again.

Something landed by his face. The bag by the smell. His own stomach foiled his attempt to play dead. He would throw the food across the room again, but the last time he'd tried, his uncle had sat down and stuffed it all into his own face in front of him, smirking the entire time. Besides, he was too tired.

"Your mom is here."

Brayton imagined jumping up and yelling obscenities, maybe even adding some growls. If he really wanted to shock her, he could probably charge into the bars and knock himself out. It was easier to just lie here though. She'd go away eventually, he hoped. He'd keep the knocking himself out plan as a backup. What he really wanted to do was disappear. He had the power, he just wasn't as practiced as Honey. That's what he should be doing instead of trying to shoot things with his eye. He could practice by sending fries to the nether.

"Brayton? Why is he laying on the ground?" his mother asked.

Brayton sniffed discretely. Was his mom truly pregnant? He couldn't smell much other than the fries next to his face. Oh well.

"I gave him a sleeping bag. It's his way of protesting. I haven't broken him yet, but we're getting there," his uncle replied.

Broken him? Is that what his uncle was doing? Did Mom know he'd been torturing him?

140

"And it stinks in here. Why does it smell so bad?"

"He had a reaction to some of the food."

"Did it have pineapple? He's allergic to pineapple."

Brayton wanted to yell 'No *mom, it had freaking magic in it!,*' but he didn't.

"Brayton, won't you sit up and talk to me? I'm sorry it had to come to this, but I didn't know what else to do."

'*You could have stayed out of my business,*' Brayton said in his head and congratulated himself on finding a way to talk to his mom without her arguing back.

"I'm worried about you dear. Your dad is worried. The whole pack is worried. We need our future alpha back."

'*Stop hating on my Luna then.*'

"Are you sure he's awake?"

Something nudged his foot. "Brayton, stop being rude to your mother."

'*She's not my mother.*' He almost grinned. Who knew not talking was the best way to have a conversation?

"Are you sure he's all right?" his mother asked.

"He's playing dead," his uncle assured her. "Trust me. I've seen it all."

"Grown men play dead? That sounds like a childish thing to do."

Now she was taunting him. He forced himself to stay calm. She didn't deserve his attention. The stupid fries though, they were harder to ignore. He discretely swallowed the saliva pooling in the back of his throat. Was he a fool to not eat them? He sniffed and focused on the more subtle smells. Human, probably whoever had handled the bag.

Money, machine oil which must be from his uncle's car, and...yeah there was something there that shouldn't be.

"Brayton! Stop acting like a child and sit up and talk to me."

He'd made her raise her voice. Ha.

Ugh, the fries. He swallowed again. He wasn't sure how much longer he could resist. He pictured the sky and vast nether beyond and sent out what must be his hundredth call. *"Honey, Honey, wherever you are, I'm sorry. It wasn't my fault. They used magic on me. Please pull me out of here. I need you."*

No response, again. He felt the tear escape the corner of his magical eye but he didn't dare wipe it away, not with his so-called family watching. They were talking to each other again so hopefully they wouldn't notice. He felt the tear tracking down his cheek and around his ear and into his hairline. Oddly, he could even feel it tracking through his hair to the steel floor of the cage below him, or maybe he imagined it. He'd been imagining a lot of things lately, like the grass on the floor and the butterflies. Why were there butterflies? It was winter, wasn't it? Maybe he'd been here longer than he realized.

Something in the air changed – a scent. It wasn't the fries though, they still smelled like grease. He pulled in a deeper breath, trying to figure out what it was. The iron of the cage still surrounded him along with the damp seeping through the concrete, but the magic; the magic was gone. He opened his eyes and studied the iron above him. It was simply black. There were no glowing colors. Finally! He rolled to his feet, slowly when he realized how dizzy he was. No food or water for four days was seriously starting to affect him.

"Brayton?"

He ignored his mom and willed his body to transform. It was slower than usual, but still a lot faster than any other wolf could do, except Honey of course.

"Why is his eye all red?" his mother asked.

"A better question is how he transformed," his uncle said.

Brayton threw back his head and let out the loudest, longest howl he could with a dry throat while yelling with all his might in his mind for his mate.

"HONEY!!!"

"What? What Brayton? What's wrong?"

She responded! He wanted to cry and laugh and bounce around, but mostly he wanted to see her. *"Get me out of here!"*

He heard a pop and felt a sting in his hip just before the smelly cement room vanished.

"Honey."

Brayton threw his paws around her and nuzzled his nose into her neck. She smelled like sleep and cement dust, but mostly, she smelled like her. He sagged against her as she wrapped her arms around his ribcage.

"What's wrong? What happened?"

"I thought you were dead and my uncle kidnapped me and put me in a cage and used magic on me and I think I told him everything but I can't remember and I haven't eaten in three or four days and I missed you."

"What is this?"

One of Honey's arms shifted and he felt another sharp pain on his hip.

"My uncle shot me with something right before I left."

143

She sniffed at something near his ear. "It doesn't smell like a sleeping dart. What does it smell like to you?"

Reluctantly, he took his nose off her neck and sniffed at the tip, then buried his nose in her neck again.

"I don't know."

"Luna Honey, who hast thee brought into mine domain?"

"My apologies Mother Lambert. This is Brayton, my chosen alpha. He woke me with a call for help and I automatically pulled him here. I did not mean to trespass on your hospitality."

Brayton lifted his head from Honey's shoulder to see who she was talking to, and noticed for the first time how bright the greens and the blues of the trees and sky were around them. It didn't look quite natural, nor did the beautiful woman dressed in the long flowing gown that reminded him of medieval times.

"He is a wolf."

"Yes."

"With a magic eye?"

"Yes. An evil wizard burned his away and my grandmother replaced it."

"He is a hybrid like thee."

"I guess," Honey said slowly.

"He is welcome then."

Brayton put his head back down with a sigh. It was hard to hold it up.

"They injected something into his blood right before I grabbed him. Can you tell what it is?"

A magical something appeared from somewhere and sniffed at the dart Honey held. The creature cocked its head like a dog and made a 'I have no idea' sound.

"Tis not magical," the woman said.

"That's what I thought."

"*Human tracking chip?*" Brayton sent.

"It has a hollow needle but unless they can make them very small, I don't think that's it. Maybe it's something unique that can be sought or found, like my blood. It was your uncle right? He wouldn't have poisoned you."

"*Don't count on it.*"

"Do you feel okay? What happened to your eye?"

"*I feel better than I did. What's wrong with my eye?*"

His stomach rumbled angrily.

"Geez." Honey reached and suddenly her backpack was in her hand. "There's some water and bars in here. Do you want to transform or shall I open them?"

"*Will you open them please?*"

"You're serious about not eating aren't you?"

"*Or drinking. I didn't trust him. The first meal made me sick. The cage was magical. I think he was putting something magical in the food too.*"

"No drinks either? Here."

She dislodged him, then pulled a camping pan out of her bag. After filling it with water for him, she proceeded to open three different bars and lay them on their wrappers where he could easily snag them.

"Mother Lambert, do you mind if I leave Brayton here while I go find him more food and try and locate Vera?"

"I doth not. I shall send mine own guardian to help thee."

145

"Thank you."

Honey pulled out another water bottle and laid it next to the bars, then scratched the sweet spot between Brayton's ears. "I'll be back. *Be very polite to her. We're floating in the nether. If she kicks you out, you'll die.*"

With those encouraging words, she vanished.

18

HONEY – DECEMBER 14 – CANADA

Honey caught herself at the last moment and stepped into the boys' restroom instead of the girls' to adjust her mustache. It was eerily empty. According to her watch, it was morning, but although the darkness outside could belong to either end of the day, the day felt like it was ending, not beginning.

"Let's check the library first."

Her companion whined.

"She's not there? We still need to go. I didn't think about the time delay when I fell asleep. I need to figure out what day it is and see what happened while I've been gone. Let me just take a quick look at a computer and then you can lead me to her."

There were a lot more people around the computers in front of the magical library entrance than anywhere else. What had happened now? She squeezed in between two groups to look at the monitors and noted it was 11:47 pm on December 14. She'd missed her own birthday.

"*In local news, four wolves from the Regis pack charged with drug trafficking were acquitted yesterday of all charges. The arresting officers, both with exemplary arrest and conviction records, are on review for illegal use of magic to plant evidence and fake memories, particularly in wolves. Rachael, what will the repercussions be if it turns out the two officers have, in fact, been using magic to send wolves to jail?*"

"It would be a mess, Greg. Every case they've been involved in would have to be reopened and investigated."

"How did this come to light?"

"(chuckle) Well, believe it not, both investigators lost their powers during the arrest of the four wolves. The cop's dashcam clearly shows the wolves kneeling, then the view flickers and ends with the investigators holding up bags of white power that are leaking everywhere. You may recall this happened over Thanksgiving and that we put out a call for any dashcam footage from passing vehicles. A truck driver heading west along that road got a clear view of the scene. His camera shows only one cop car when there should have been two, and a white wolf or dog wearing a harness. Neither the investigators nor the wolves remember the animal."

"What do you mean, lost their powers Rachael?"

"They were bound, Greg, and so far no one has been able to unbind them. One witch went so far as to say they'd been cursed."

"Any idea who bound them?"

"Not yet, Greg, but the Canadian counsel has requested the aid of US witch Silvia Cromwell, who is internationally known for her ability to identify the casters of spells. She was scheduled to come this week but the event in Boston delayed her."

"Understandably. Keep us informed."

"Do you mind? I can't see," a girl complained at Honey.

"Sorry," she said in her deepest voice and backed away.

How fast would they figure out she was the one who bound the cops. If Silvia Cromwell had been exposed to her signature in Boston, it probably wouldn't take long at all. She might need to avoid Canada for a while.

She waited until she was back outside and free of the crowd before whispering to the guardian jogging next to her,

"Okay, let's get some food before all the restaurants close, then maybe you can guide me to Vera?"

Her friend yipped.

There weren't many people on the bus downtown, just her, a trio of giggling girls, a young man with a bush of hair and a Harry Potter-esk scarf scrolling on his phone, and a stern looking woman who perused Honey from the top of her beanie to the toe of the nice motorcycle boots Brayton had provided her with. Honey channeled her inner Nathan and raised a semi-flirtatious eyebrow at the woman, then slid into her seat like she imagined he would.

The woman and the girls got off at the same stop she did. Honey didn't like the way the woman was watching her. Had her eyebrow been too flirtatious? She should ask Nathan for tips the next time she saw him. He'd get a kick out of that.

Pretending to ignore them all, she headed for the closest pizza place. Concernedly, the woman followed, but instead of going into the restaurant, she stopped to converse with a guy leaning against a lamppost. That was weird. It was cold and dark outside. Why would a guy be leaning against a lamppost at midnight? Scratch that. Now it was the woman.

"Can I help you?" the guy at the counter asked.

"Large pepperoni. Is that a bus stop?" she asked, pointing over her shoulder to the woman outside. "Seems like a cold place to wait."

"Nah." He leaned closer when he handed her the receipt. "They're looking for Honey Smith."

She could smell the wolf on him, so she asked, "The hybrid?"

"Yeah."

149

She didn't want to appear too dumb, so she kept her question simple. "Here?"

"You see the news?"

"Not for a few days. Finals."

"She set off a bomb in a library in Boston."

Honey barely kept herself from correcting the guy. "Why?"

He shrugged. "Why do all terrorists do what they do?"

She was a terrorist now? Great. "Was anyone hurt?"

"A few I think, but no deaths."

That must have been the guards. "Why are they looking for her here if she blew up a library in Boston?"

"Dunno, maybe they got a tip."

"They think she'd hide here? Weird."

"Yeah."

Fudge. If Ms. Cromwell was still in the US, that meant the witches must have made the connection between the things taken and Vera. Contacting Vera just got a lot harder. Honey leaned against the wall where she could keep an eye on the counter, the front door, and the lamppost outside.

"*I think you're going to have to bring Vera to me. Can you do that?*" she sent to the invisible guardian on her shoulder.

It made a questioning sound.

"*Not here. I mean can you take her to the pendant, but only if she's alone or if just Michael is with her and not yet. Let me get close to where she's staying so I can bring her back later.*"

Her friend yipped a yes.

Ten minutes later she left with her hot pizza and a pocket full of napkins.

"Is she close or should I take a bus?" she whispered to the spell once she was outside.

The spell creature leaped to the ground and took off, directly past the woman standing next to the pole.

Honey pretended not to see the woman and walked like she had a purpose. The woman's magic reached out and brushed against Honey's shields when she got close. With the wind and her shields so thick, Honey couldn't smell it well, but whatever the woman's power was, it wasn't pleasant. Should she ignore it or react? Under normal circumstances, she'd ignore it, maybe, but she was playing a part. Honey stopped beside the woman and turned her head just enough to catch her eye.

"I've got plans for tonight," Honey lifted her pizza, "and you're a little old for me, but I'm always up for new things. You come here often?"

"You need to work on your pick-up lines. Get out of here."

Honey made sure to cackle guyishly while she walked away.

Two blocks later, the guardian plopped its little rear onto the cold sidewalk in front of a big house. She was sure it looked like any other house to humans, but with her magic sight, she could see the lines of magic all over it. One even flowed from the door to a dark car with a faint glow coming from the back seat. She might have felt sorry for the guy watching the house in the cold if it wasn't her he was trying to catch.

She'd paused. To waylay suspicion from the guy watching the house, she pretended to pull a phone out of her pocket and read it, then marched past the house. Another block and a turn later, she dropped her glove between a car and the curb.

"Go," she whispered to the spell-dog, then planted an anchor on the curb, picked up her glove, and sent herself and her pizza to the nether.

Her lips landed on Brayton's still fuzzy cheek. He still hadn't transformed? Did he feel that weak?

"That was fast," he sent. Honey noted he'd only eaten one bar, but the hour she'd been gone would have been less than a minute here.

Brayton snorted in her head. *"Nice beard."*

"Thank you."

She rubbed his big head, then opened the lid to the pizza box so he could get to it. "Do you want pizza?"

"I would love pizza."

"Don't eat too fast."

"I know. Thank you. You take a piece first."

"I didn't poison it!"

"You need to eat too."

He wasn't wrong. Honey grabbed a piece then straightened to face the girl waiting impatiently in a warm-looking set of plaid pajamas with her hands firmly on her hips. "Hi Vera."

"Did you set off a bomb in the library?"

"No." Honey took a bite and closed her eyes while the cheesy pepperoniness bathed her tongue.

"Were you there when it happened?"

She swallowed. "Yes."

"Did you get hurt?"

"No. I got lucky. I ducked and the bomb fell behind a desk. The desk blocked the blast."

Brayton's head popped up and she had to suppress a giggle at the pizza sauce all over his muzzle. "*What is she talking about?*"

"*I'll explain later.*"

"Why were you in the library?" Vera asked. "I thought you were getting us a boat to go to the ocean or something."

"I was, but when I landed in Boston, the guardian bit me, then Mother Lambert asked me to retrieve your things and give them to you. In return, she promised to have the guardian retrieve the curse tablet. I thought that would be easier than finding a boat and twenty witches, so I agreed. I'm not sure it was a good deal or not considering someone figured out how to portal a bomb at me while I was there and now everyone thinks I'm a terrorist."

"I don't think you're a terrorist," Vera said.

"*Someone threw a bomb at you?*" Brayton growled at the same time.

"*I'm okay,*" Honey sent when Brayton abandoned his pizza to sniff at her. "Eat."

To Vera, she said, "You're the only one. Anyway, I am officially presenting you your things. Where do you want them?"

"I can't take them right now. They're watching me."

"I could put them with the books. After the bomb disaster I figured the witches would put two and four together and check your house again, so I moved them into the pirate ship. Oh, I know! I'll make a stash charm for you and anchor it to the boat, so whenever you're ready you can pull it out of the nether yourself."

"Um, do you have something other than a boat, like maybe a moving truck?"

Honey chuckled. "I do not have a truck, but I can move everything into one if you find one."

"Yes, please, and you can make the key into a charm."

"Sure."

Honey tried to take another bite, but her arms were abruptly pinned in a very tight hug.

"I'm so glad you're okay. I didn't know what to think. The news said your magical signature was all over the blast site. I was afraid you'd blown yourself up."

"Why would I do that?"

Vera released Honey with a shrug. "Spell gone wrong maybe? I singed my eyebrows off once."

Honey glanced at Vera's eyebrows. She did have some. "How? You're a water witch."

"I know! See, it can happen to anyone." She turned to the spell woman. "Mother Lambert, Honey has fulfilled her side of the bargain. Send your guardian to retrieve the curse."

"She hast to give thee the key. Thee must have full control of everything before I doth so."

Vera shook her head firmly. "No. They are watching me and it may take days or weeks or even months to obtain a van. I am satisfied that she has removed the items."

"They must be in thy possession first," the spell woman said stubbornly. "People are trying to dispatch her. Should she die, all shall be lost in the nether forever."

154

Honey kicked herself for being so lazy. She'd known the ship wasn't the best place to store things. "I have an idea, but it might take a while to put together," Honey said. "I'll take you back for now. Once I get the key ready, I'll send the guardian after you again. Is that okay?" she asked both women.

The spell-woman gave a sharp nod. Vera's was more reluctant.

"Good. Come on Vera. Hopefully it's still dark. There's a time delay here. More than an hour passes for every minute here."

Her eyes grew big. "Really? Hurry then. I don't want people to see me in my pajamas."

"They're cute pajamas."

Vera looked down at herself. "You think so? Michael bought them for me. It's the first time I've had some. Aunt Philomena always made me wear gowns."

"Art thee yet married?" the spell woman queried.

Vera held up her hand and wiggled her finger to show off the ring Honey hadn't noticed the last time they'd talked. "We are engaged. We are only awaiting approval from Madame Wixx."

"Thee dost not need her approval. Thou art a Lambert!"

"The only Lambert. It's better to forge bridges than to burn them, don't you think?"

The spell woman squinted at Vera, but she didn't disagree.

Honey grabbed Vera's hand and tugged her down. A moment later, they were both squatting behind the car where Honey had planted her anchor on the curb. The sky was still dark except for the full moon right about their heads.

"Wow. That's a bright moon," Vera commented.

Honey's skin started tingling. She quickly looked around but she couldn't see anything.

"Run Vera. Run that way, now! I think there's another bomb." Honey ran in the opposite direction. As soon as she cleared the branches of the overhanging tree and stepped into the full light of the moon her skin went from tingly to something else entirely. It felt like she was standing under the summer sun instead of a winter moon.

"Not here. Not here," she whispered, willing the moon to listen. "Not in town. Not where people can see."

The moon ignored her. She was trapped in the beams, unable to run, unable to travel. The light soaked into her skin, and even though only her face and hands were showing, she could feel it on every part of her as if she stood in wolf form instead of human.

Why was this happening? She was nearly certain it didn't happen to all Lunas every time there was a full moon, at least it hadn't happened to Brayton's mom that one time they'd run together. Brayton would know, but was it safe for him to be there? The moon didn't care. It wanted her alpha. She could feel it. Honey pulled him out of the nether to float/stand beside her.

He transformed from his light gray wolf into clothes she'd never seen before. They looked like something a fairy tale prince would wear except glowing. He smiled and pushed her long hair back from her face, her long silver hair. What was going on?

"I think the moon wants us to finish what we started last month," Brayton said softly, "and now I can."

He kissed her in the center of her forehead. "I accept you into my pack." He kissed the right side of her head, "and I accept you as my Luna." He kissed the left side, "and as my mate," he kissed the center one more time, "for now and forever more."

He couldn't do that. He shouldn't do that. "Brayton."

"Shh, it will be all right." He pressed his lips against hers.

She'd enjoyed kissing him before, but this was something else. Her whole body felt more alive than it ever had before. She could feel him almost as much as she felt herself. His mind was beginning to show damage from being outside of a pack, but she fixed it easily, and the foreign substance in his blood she sent away with a thought. The love he had for her was almost overwhelming yet sweet and beautiful. It didn't matter that she was only sixteen. She could spend a lifetime with this boy who was growing into a wonderful man. She'd known it for months. He truly was her fated. She pulled her lips from his and moved them to his forehead.

"I accept you as my alpha, Brayton." She moved to the right and planted a second kiss, "and as my mate," she planted the third kiss on the left, "for now and forever more."

"I love you Honey," Brayton said softly, pressing his forehead against hers.

"I love you too."

She faintly registered that they were beginning to sink back to the ground and that outside of the bright moonlight that still surrounded them, ominous shadows shifted and moved.

She put her lips back on Brayton's and mumbled. "Hold your breath."

19

BRAYTON – DECEMBER 14 – NETHER

"Thou art back again?"

"Sorry to intrude Mother Lambert. We ran into a little issue," Honey said politely. "Is the guardian following Vera? I couldn't stay to make sure she got home safely."

The spell woman frowned and scrutinized the two of them. "Thou art glowing, and thy stars are three." She lifted her hand toward Brayton's head but stopped short of touching it. "Thou hast won her heart."

He looked down worriedly at Honey. Had he dreamed what had just happened?

Honey beamed up at him, making his chest feel like it was going to explode with happiness. "Thou hast."

"Thou art mates," the woman stated.

"Yep. The moon kind of insisted," Honey said, still smiling at him. She was glowing like the moon itself and, thank goodness, had lost the beard.

"A Celestial Alpha. Interesting." Mother Lambert paused. "Vera is back in her room."

"I think I know where an abandoned bus is," Honey said. "I could get that and put her things in it until she's ready for them. It won't tip over like a boat."

"What about the people sending bombs after you," Brayton asked. "Shouldn't you make a protection spell against that?"

"It wasn't a seeking spell," the spell woman stated. "If so, it wouldst have hit the outside of the building. I wouldst guess it was a portal spell tuned to thy blood."

Honey sighed. "Okay, so how do I protect against that? I already have a portal-blocking spell and I know that works."

"That tis your magic, is it not?" Mother Lambert said. "Protection? All spells were created by someone."

"True." Honey made a face and rubbed her forehead. "I'm sure I can come up with something, but my brain is still buzzing from all that magic."

She looked tired.

Brayton pulled her into his arms. She smelled like winter air and moon magic mixed with her own unique magical scent that always made his stomach dance. The dress the moon had gifted to her made her look like a fairytale woodland creature with her bouncy, curly hair which had thankfully reverted to its normal beautiful brown.

"Maybe you don't need to do anything," he threw out. "What if we just wait here a couple of hours? People will get tired of searching for you eventually and I wouldn't mind finishing the pizza." Later. He was feeling a little too full at the moment.

"Don't you still have finals?"

He shook his head against the soft curls under his own. "Mom had me kidnapped before I could take them. It's all right," he said when she opened her mouth to rant. "I don't care about college as much as I care about you. Once we get

159

through this, we can go to college together, or we can skip it and open a business together or you can go to college and I'll support you. It doesn't matter as long as we're together."

"But your pack...won't it be easier to run if you have the proper education?"

"I've been learning how to run a pack since I could walk. The degree is only icing. It's more to prove I have enough brainpower to complete a task than anything. What you want to learn," he continued before she could protest, "definitely calls for more education."

"I probably won't get to be a scientist," she admitted with a sigh.

"I think you can be whatever you want. It just depends how determined you are."

Honey stepped back and looked down at her dress. "Well, I can't do anything until I get Vera's stuff sorted, so I better get that done first. It won't take long once I snag the bus. What on Earth am I wearing?"

"Tis beautiful," the spell woman said. "It's moon silk. Very rare. I've only heard of it ere now."

"Where did it come from? I'm pretty sure the moon can't make clothes."

"It's not of fabric. It's of magic. Tis a gift."

"What am I supposed to do with it?"

"Wear it."

"But I can't..."

"Honey," Brayton said, grabbing her hand. "What if you wait a little before finishing your tasks? You said there's a time delay between here and earth. How much of a delay?"

"If we spent 4.5 days here, that would equal about a year on earth."

"A year?" He hadn't realized it was so different. 4.5 days was nothing compared to a year. "Would it hurt to wait that long?"

"You think I should wait a year?" she asked incredulously.

"Think about it. There's a lot of heat on Vera right now and on you. By next December people will have forgotten all about her and whoever is trying to throw things at you will definitely get tired of trying after a year. It will only be a few days for us."

"What about your family and friends? What about your mom?"

Brayton shook his head. "It will be hard on them, but maybe we can get a message to my dad not to worry. It will serve mom right though."

"Don't be like that. You know she loves you."

"I know." It was his turn to sigh.

"It won't be as easy as you think. There are no bathrooms here and I don't have enough food and I don't know that Mother Lambert wants us to stay here that long, plus there won't be much to do," Honey said, looking around.

"Thou art welcome," the spell woman said graciously, "as long as thou take care of the issues thou hast made mention of. There is plenty of magic hither, and the amount thou are both expelling is sufficient to supplement mine power for many days." She waved her arm toward the trees. "The land goes as far as thou desire. Thou canst explore, or thou canst work on thy spell."

161

"What about Vera," Honey asked. "She will be expecting to hear from me."

"We shall speak to her after the 'heat' as thou named it hath cooled. Mine guardian will keep watch over her."

"I suppose we can get some MREs," Honey said thoughtfully, "and a camping toilet."

"Not MREs," Brayton said quickly.

She gave him an understanding look. "Fine, no MREs."

He couldn't help himself. He pulled her closer again. "I love you."

She didn't say it, but she snuggled into him with a soft sigh. "We can get what we need at Walmart. I know where one is."

"Let's wait as long as we can."

"Okay."

20

BRAYTON – DECEMBER 13 – A YEAR LATER

It was the best 4.5 days he'd ever had. They ran, they swam, they joked, she crafted charms, they even did a little cuddling, although not for long. They were both too aware the spell witch was probably watching. On the fifth day, Honey took him to the abandoned bus in Australia which handily still had a stable floor. After they had pushed the garbage out, she took the bus back to the nether, had it filled with books and artifacts in seconds, and the next thing he knew, they were in a bright room with a partially built crib and bags of baby things.

"Vera, are you here?" Honey called out.

"Coming. I'm coming," a female voice called from somewhere far away. Several seconds later, a panting Vera was in the room. Her slim figure now sported an obvious bump. She looked fresh out of the fifties with her colorful maternity dress and her hair up in a kerchief. She even had a duster in her hand.

"You look happy," Honey said.

Vera tossed the duster on the floor and rushed to give Honey a hug. "I am. Oh my gosh, you look exactly the same as you did last year."

"It's only been four days."

"For you maybe." Vera rubbed her belly. "Clearly a little longer for me." Releasing Honey, she stepped in front of Brayton and offered him a hand. "Alpha Brayton."

He took her hand but pulled her close enough to squeeze her shoulders. Her scent reminded him of babies and a crystal-clear brook that bubbled out of the ground on his family's pack lands. "Wolves like hugs."

"Oh!" she squeaked. "I didn't know."

"And here is your key." Honey said, producing the one she'd bought at Walmart and then painted with swirls of blue and colorful flowers with a flourish. She'd even tied a ribbon at the top. He hadn't realized until then that she was artistic, although it didn't surprise him. "I doubt the bus has an engine, so you only need to tap where you want the front of the hood to sit and it will appear. Make sure you tap high enough."

"Can I send it back once it's empty?"

"Yep."

Vera visibly relaxed. "Oh good. Our yard isn't big enough to hide something like that."

"Your house looks beautiful."

"It is! It was built in 1907 and has the original stained glass and pocket doors and some hand painted frescoes. They call this style a 'New Art' design. Five bedrooms, four bathrooms, wood floors. You should see the stairs in the entry, and the woodwork in the dining room is just amazing. Come on, I'll give you the tour. Your timing is perfect." She started down the stairs. "Michael just finished painting the library."

"Are you going to start another school?"

164

"I wasn't, but people kept asking so we're offering our first classes in January. We're only going to teach – no boarders for now. We've already got twenty students signed up."

"When is the baby due?" Honey asked.

"April. I might even call her April," Vera said, rubbing her belly fondly.

"That's pretty."

"What did you do with the old house," Brayton asked.

Vera wrinkled her nose. "It's still sitting there. I have to make sure everything magical is gone before I put it up for sale and … I just can't go in there."

"We could look," Honey volunteered.

"There's a lot of hidden stuff."

"We can go with you, for support."

"Oh, you are," Vera turned to face them, and Brayton was concerned to see her eyes brimming with tears, "you are the kindest person, Honey." She engulfed Honey in another hug, then stepped back with a sniff and wiped the tears off her face. "Don't mind me. It's a pregnancy thing."

They followed her into what Brayton guessed was the dining room due to the large table. The room reminded him of a French restaurant he'd eaten in once with the dark wood trim and plaster walls and the huge fireplace in which a small fire was burning. Vera went to the built-in hutch that was set at an angle in the corner and picked up a small object which she offered to Honey.

"Now don't be mad," Vera said as Honey took it. "She said she only wanted to talk to you and it was the only way we could get her approval."

"Mad about what?"

Brayton smelled the magic right before the floor opened underneath him and he and Honey fell into the dark. He grabbed Honey's arm about the same time his feet landed on something solid. With two blinks, he saw what his nose had already told them. Honey's transparent golden shield surrounded them both. Beyond that was a dim room. It was somewhat similar to the one they'd just left in that it had a lot of woodwork and plaster, but it looked even older and was filled with clutter.

"Where are we?"

"Looks like the library in Indiana," Honey said bemusedly.

"The witch library?"

"I did not say that."

The door flew open and the stern librarian who'd helped arrange meetings with Honey's grandmother when he had his eye fixed rushed into the room. "Honey! You're alive."

"You knew that. My leaf is still on the tree."

"and Brayton Mooney, the wolf," the librarian finished.

"Ms. Carrier."

The woman straightened determinedly. "Wolves are not allowed in the library."

Brayton wasn't sure what was going on, but the creaking and moaning the library started making couldn't be good.

"If you harm him, I'll tear down every protection you have. You hear that library," Honey yelled at the room, "I don't want to hurt you, but I will if you hurt him."

A small 'shing' made Brayton look up. Before he could truly comprehend what was happening, the vision in his magical eye turned red and the thing that had been about to

166

strike him in the face fell at his feet. It looked like a small bumble bee.

"I warned you," Honey growled. Brayton felt the power next to him increase, but he didn't dare take his eyes off the library.

"It didn't hurt him! It was a test. Just a test," Ms. Carrier squealed. "Stand down, library. Stand down. He has magic."

"All wolves have magic," Honey said beside him.

"Witch magic," Ms. Carrier corrected.

"Of course he does," a second voice proclaimed fondly. Rachel Wixx strode through the open door all smiles, followed by a taller, leaner, older, and sterner woman. "Honey, my dear, and my lovely alpha-in-law."

"Grandmother!"

To Brayton's surprise, Honey didn't drop her shields.

"Rachel, enough of that nonsense," the older woman scolded Honey's grandmother. "Ms. Carrier, why is there a wolf in the library?"

"It let him in. I had nothing to do with it."

"Exile him."

"He goes, I go. Just say what you wanted to say, Great-Grandmother," Honey demanded.

"You think you are more powerful than all your ancestors combined?" the older lady chuckled. "Ms. Carrier."

Honey pulled Brayton closer so that they were basically embracing. Ms. Carrier stepped forward and pointed the huge ring on her finger at him. "Brayton Mooney, you are hereby exiled from the library."

The librarian sounded very grand. He wouldn't have been surprised to find himself in the middle of a parched plain with

167

vultures flying overhead, but nothing happened. Honey's shields didn't even flicker.

"What's wrong with the ring? Did you drop it?" the old woman demanded.

"No! It's fine. It worked the last time."

The old woman turned on Rachel Wixx who was watching everything with an amused smile. "Daughter! What did you do?"

"I didn't do anything."

"Tell me what you know," the older woman demanded.

Brayton caught a cloying scent over the rest of the near-overwhelming magical stench of the library.

"That's not his name. He's Honey's mate, which is even deeper than husband. That means he has her name. The thing is," Rachel Wixx continued while the librarian opened her mouth again, "I'm not sure what Honey's name truly is."

"She is a Wixx," the old woman declared.

"Then he is too. He belongs here as much as the next man."

"How did you know he is my mate?" Honey asked.

"The whole world knows," Rachel replied with a chuckle. "You were caught on film a year ago, right before you vanished. Do you still have the moon silk?"

"Yes."

"Did you know it has many healing properties? I have a book I can lend you."

"Rachel, not now," her mother snapped.

"Why are we here?" Honey asked.

"My mother has decided she wants you to be her successor," Rachel Wixx said when no one else did.

"Me? The hybrid?"

"Yes," the older lady sniffed. "You are more powerful than all of your featherbrained cousins. Your impure blood will make it difficult to arrange a good match, but I've already found a few gentlemen who have expressed interest."

"A match?"

"It is traditional for the successor to marry a male who also exhibits strong powers. That's how we keep the main bloodline strong," Rachel explained.

"I'm basically already married, besides, look how good your matchmaking turned out for my mom. No thank you."

"You are *not* married!" the older Wixx woman declared. "Not with my approval."

"No, we had the moon's approval. It kind of insisted."

"Mother, I told you…"

"Hush, Rachel!"

The kind woman's mouth snapped shut and she ducked her head like some kind of servant. She didn't want to though. Brayton could see the invisible lines of magic forcing her mouth shut and her head down. No one should treat a kind old woman like that, especially her own mother. "Stop!" he growled, letting his alpha power lose. "Don't you ever use your magic on her again!"

The old woman's eyes widened and she swayed like she'd been hit with a wave, which he supposed, she had. She recovered quickly though and turned on her daughter again.

"Rachel, touch your toes!"

Mrs. Wixx looked down at her feet, then back up and beamed at Brayton. "No. Mother."

"What kind of spell is this?" the old woman demanded.

"Told you wolves had magic," Honey smirked.

The old woman jabbed a finger at Honey. "You are my successor. And you," she pointed at Brayton. Her lips pressed together like they were fighting the words trying to come out. They lost. "Are her consort. I expect you to present yourselves to the library for training once you break that moon-damned curse. Now, begone with you, and don't you dare get caught!"

"O-kay." Honey shared a confused look with Brayton while the older woman stormed out.

"Nicely done," Rachael Wixx beamed at them. "Ms. Carrier, you should probably keep an eye on Mother if there are any students about. I'm not sure of her mood."

"Right. Good point." The librarian hesitated a moment, and then bowed her head. "Honey, I just want to say, I'm sorry for any misunderstanding between us. I wouldn't have turned you in. I'm glad you're okay."

Honey surprised Brayton by dropping her shields and running across the room to pull the librarian into a tight hug. The librarian looked surprised too.

"I'm so glad to hear that. I wanted to be friends with you because you were friends with Mom, but I was afraid. Maybe now we can be."

"Well," the librarian stepped back and adjusted her shirt, "I'm old enough to be your mother, but we'll see."

"She gets a hug but I don't?" Mrs. Wixx complained, opening her arms.

Honey spun around and ran into her grandmother's arms.

"Mmm, that's what I've been missing. As soon as you get rid of that curse, you're moving in with me. I expect at least one hug every morning."

"What about Brayton?"

"He can live there too."

"Umm," he started.

"Or, you could come live with us as soon as we find a place," Honey said, kissing her grandmother on the top of the head. "We haven't seen his family yet, and he's supposed to be the alpha eventually, so we need to check on that too."

"Speaking of my family," Brayton said, "have you heard anything about them? Was my mother truly pregnant?"

"I'm sorry Brayton," Mrs. Wixx began with a mournful tone that made his heart nearly stop, "I haven't heard anything for months. Your mom contacted me several times last winter and once in the summer asking if I'd heard from you but that's it. Your uncle though," Mrs. Wixx said to Honey, "informed me last December that his wife had a healthy baby boy, and to pass it on to you if I saw you."

"That's wonderful news," Honey grinned. "I can't wait to meet him."

"I think he might have been born on your birthday. Oh my goodness," Mrs. Wixx said, slapping her hand over her mouth. "Today is your birthday. You're seventeen today, right?"

"No, I'm actually sixteen today. I missed my birthday last year."

Her grandmother shook her head. "It doesn't work that way dear, if so, I'd be twenty years younger."

"Really? You've missed that many birthdays?"

171

Rachael dismissed her concern with a wave. "Cake goes right to my hips and I'd rather not keep count of the years."

"When is your birthday?"

"You don't need to know. Anyway, I got you a present. I actually got it last year, but since I never saw you, ah-hem, I never got to give it to you. You stay right here and I'll go get it."

"So, this is the witch library," Brayton said, looking around once they were alone. "It looks very…witchy."

Honey punched him. "Silly."

He shook a finger at her. "Now listen you…"

Sharp points, like a small dog was biting him, stabbed into his finger and the library disappeared.

21

HONEY – DECEMBER 13 – TEXAS

"There it tis, take it." The spell woman nodded at a dirty lump of gray laying in the overly bright grass.

Honey put her hand over it to inspected it for traps before touching it. She had begun to trust the Lambert women, but no longer. Vera's betrayal stung, even if she didn't mean any harm. She and Brayton had skipped a year of everyone's lives to start afresh and already the advantage was lost.

"Do not be harsh on Vera. She didst what she had to, to continue our line," the spell woman said.

"I know," Honey said.

"Thou shall forgive her."

"I will consider it."

"She needs thy friendship."

"I don't like being used and thrown away."

"Thou needst her too."

"I know," Honey acknowledged. She was well aware of how unique and precious true friends were. She wondered if she still had any beyond Brayton.

"Hast thou retrieved the fifth tablet?" the woman asked.

"I read it was destroyed and I didn't find it when I used the quaerere map."

"Those only work in the physical realm."

"You think it's in the nether?"

"Thou dost not?"

Her heart fell. How was she supposed to find such a small thing in the huge nether with so much other junk floating around in the magical soup? "Are there maps to the nether so I can scry for it like I did the others?"

"Thou knowest the answer."

She did. It was no. You couldn't map soup. Ugh, if she had known, she wouldn't have wasted the last few days basically vacationing. "I could try a summoning spell."

"Thou could," the woman agreed.

It wouldn't be a very strong one considering she was only one person, well, maybe two. She looked up at Brayton who was watching the interaction with such love and concern, her stomach went all mushy on her. Would his magic work like witch magic?

"We'll need some supplies."

"Vera will have them."

Abruptly, they were in a yard with real grass and a large rusty bus and a young man carrying a book of boxes. He stopped and gaped for a moment, "Honey?"

"Hi Michael. Congratulations on the baby."

He set the books on the ground, then rushed over and swept her into a hug. "You survived Madame Wixx."

She didn't hug him back. "You knew about that?"

He released her and stepped back with his head hung. "I did. I'm sorry. We didn't want to agree but it was the only way to get her approval and she promised she wouldn't hurt you and," he raised his head, "we knew you could handle it."

"You could have warned me, or at least waited until I'd finished with the curse. Now people know we're back. You totally negated our reason for staying away for a year!"

He ducked his head again. "I'm sorry. You're right. We should have waited. I don't know why we didn't think of that."

Brayton's warm hand slipped around her own. "Compulsion I bet. That's Madame Wixx's power, right?"

Honey took a deep breath and released some of her anger with a sigh. "Right. It wasn't completely your fault Michael. She's just…ugh."

Michael raised his head cautiously. "Did she try to kill you?"

"No, she tried to kill Brayton though."

"Oh. Why?"

"She wanted to pair me with someone else."

He frowned. "Why? Why would she…" His eyes got wide. "She wants you to be her successor!"

"Yes. How did you know?"

"Because that's all anyone has been talking about for months. Once it came out that your mom was dead and that you exist but weren't all witch, some of the different Wixx factions started pressuring Madame Wixx to name her heir, one of my aunts in particular," he rolled his eyes. "She thinks your existence is proof that it's time to hand over the baton to younger blood who can control their offspring, her words, but no one is strong enough to force Madame Wixx down. My aunt is going to flip when she hears." He sobered. "No one is going to accept you. They're all going to fight it. Madame Wixx has to know that."

"I bet that's why she's doing it," Brayton said. "If Honey dies, it gets rid of a problem, but if she lives, the Wixx clan will have the strongest leader in generations."

"I didn't agree," Honey pointed out.

"Doesn't matter," Michael said. "Once she announces it, there will be a target on your back."

"I already have a target on my back."

She had hoped though, that after she broke the curse, the target would fade and she'd be able to live like a normal person.

Brayton tugged her into a hug. "Hey. No matter what happens, I'm with you. We'll figure it out."

"Honey, Brayton, you're back!" Vera called behind them. "I'm so glad. Did everything go okay? What did Madame Wixx want?"

She was smiling like she hadn't just sent her and Brayton off to possible death. Was she that naive or did she not care? Honey shook her head. "It doesn't matter. Mother Lambert said you'd have supplies to do a summoning."

"Oh, sure," the young woman nodded.

"And would you perhaps have a portal that *doesn't* send me someplace I don't want to go?"

Vera's smile faltered. "Yes, yes of course. Come inside. I'll get everything you need. Was Mother Lambert not able to retrieve the tablet?" she asked while they walked across the yard.

"She was, but technically there's still one missing. I just want to make absolutely sure it's not out there somewhere."

"Oh!" she smiled brightly up at Honey, "You'll need my help then. I know some other witches who can help too. If you put on a disguise, they won't be any wiser."

"I'll keep that in mind, but I want to try by myself first. There will be less chance of exposing myself that way or of people turning on me."

"Sure," Vera said with a hint of sadness. "I understand."

Honey suspected she wasn't as sad as she was acting, but her nose told her it wasn't all fake. "Vera, your house is lovely. Can we get the rest of the tour before we leave?"

Vera immediately brightened at Honey's overture of friendship. "Yes!"

22

BRAYTON – DECEMBER 13 – NETHER

Brayton held up the camping lantern Honey had handed him and peered into the murky nether while she unpacked the summoning kit Vera had loaned her. The light traveled just far enough for him to make out the edge of the pirate ship deck all around them and a few things floating beyond. It was unnerving to think that how often he'd floated in that murk. Sometimes it truly was better not to know.

Honey adjusted his arm so the light fell on the mat printed with the circle/star thing witches liked to use. Did the colorful crystals she'd placed at the star's points actually do anything or were they pretty weights? She'd arranged the four curse tables in a square shape around the inside of the star. Those, at least, made sense. Honey gave a little nod to herself, then smiled at him, and suddenly they were back behind the bus in Vera's yard.

Still smiling, she took a deep breath. "Okay, one more trip. You ready for this?"

"I just stand there, right?"

"No. You have to think about what we want. No, better, visualize the fifth piece showing up in the center of the star. Ooo, even better, use your alpha power and command it to show up."

"You have no idea what you're doing, do you?"

"Nope, but it won't hurt to try."

He leaned in and kissed her cheek. "I love how optimistic you are."

"Flatterer."

He turned his face toward her lips, hoping she'd get the hint. She did. It didn't last long though. She pulled away, her eyes bright with anticipation.

"Let's get this done."

A moment later, the ship was again under their feet. He lifted the lantern and nearly screamed at the sightless face directly in front of him. Not sightless. Wooden. Honey simply shook her head and gave the wooden woman a little push so that she floated away from the center of the circle.

Turning to him, she sent *"Ready?"*

He gave a thumbs up.

The wooden woman was already in the center of the circle again.

"That's odd," Honey sent.

Brayton pointed at the wooden woman and made a questioning gesture.

"I don't know who she is, but she did show me this ship."

She pulled the woman out of the circle and held on to her this time. *"Maybe she wants to help with the summoning."*

Brayton raised an eyebrow at her.

"What? It could happen. You stayed for nearly five days in a necklace."

That was true. He blinked twice to see if the statue looked magical. The hair on the back of his neck raised to nearly painful points when he saw the sinister red glow surrounding her. He grabbed Honey's arm and jerked her toward him, surprising her so much she let go of the statue. He blatantly winked twice with his magic eye when Honey frowned at him and pointed to the woman. Honey turned her head, but instead of scooting away from the statue, she grabbed it and him, and pulled them both out the nether.

Before he could ask what she was doing, Honey lifted her finger, now a claw, and passed it through the air in front of the woman. The rough face immediately began to turn smoother and lighter, the detailed wooden dress became actual fabric, and the eyes blinked. The head, now sporting thick, wavy brown hair that trailed down the woman's back, turned. A living, breathing young woman, perhaps in her early twenties, stood before them.

Before Brayton thought to react, or even if he should react, the woman lunged and pulled Honey into a hug.

"You saved me! Thank you!"

"Who are you?" Honey asked.

The woman released her and gave a little curtsy. "Theodosia Wixx. And you are?"

"Honey."

The woman cocked her head. "No surname?"

"I've gone by Smith most of my life, but my mother was a Wixx."

"I knew it! I knew we were related!" She looked Honey up and down, then looked all around. "Where are we?"

"Texas."

The woman frowned. "I do not know of this place."

"What year were you born?" Honey asked.

"1733. What year is it now?"

180

"2024."

"Five," Brayton corrected.

Honey nodded, "Oh, right."

"I was gone that long? It did not seem so. I would have guessed a few years, not hundreds."

"Time passes much slower in the nether. You were cursed. Why?"

The young woman lifted her arms and opened her hands. Each one held half of a flat, gray metal tablet. "I was trying to destroy this. I bent it to fit it into my crucible, and the next thing I knew, I was in darkness and unable to move or breath."

"She was right. There is a protection curse on the tablets," Honey hummed.

"Who was right," Brayton demanded.

"Mother Lambert. Don't worry Brayton, I got this." Honey extended her hands toward the woman and Brayton barely kept himself from grabbing them and jerking them back. "May I?"

"You need to finish this," the woman said, handing the pieces of the curse table to her.

"That's exactly what I plan to do."

"No, now. You don't have much time."

Before Brayton could ask what she meant, Honey grabbed his and the woman's arm. "Then let's go."

A moment later they were in the nether again. Honey extended her hand and grabbed the bag that flew into it, then before Brayton could blink, they were standing next to an evergreen tree in the middle of a snowy field in the near dark under less than half a moon.

Brayton shivered. "Where are we?"

"Scotland. I thought it would be good if we could break the curse where it was set," Honey explained.

"In Scotland?" the woman asked.

"No, further south." Honey pulled out the sand-dollar portal shell Vera had given her and sniffed it.

"What's wrong?" Brayton asked.

"I'm just checking. It smells like a portal. I was warned someone would betray me." Honey turned to the woman beside her. "That was you, wasn't it, who wrote down the warning?"

"Yes."

"Who was it or is it yet to happen?"

Brayton didn't like the way the woman's eyes flicked to him, then back to Honey before she said, "It has not happened yet."

"I would never betray her. She is my mate and Luna," Brayton protested.

"I did not see who it was. I only saw the outcome."

The sorrowful look she gave didn't bode well.

"What happens?" Brayton demanded.

"Maybe nothing. Forward sight is a tricky thing. Just be wary."

"Is the portal safe at least?" Honey asked. "We could try to destroy them here."

"It happens right after the last tablet is destroyed."

"Let's go then."

"Wait!" Brayton said, grabbing Honey's arm so she wouldn't activate the portal. "Tell us everything you see so we can be prepared."

"Blood."

"What causes it?" he asked.

"I don't know, I didn't see. I just saw it pouring from her chest."

He turned to Honey. He couldn't have stopped shaking his head if he wanted to. "No. You can't do this Honey."

"What else did you see," Honey asked. "Was it dark, lights, was there snow or rain, anything?"

"Lots of white," she looked around, "but not here. There was no tree."

"Then we'll do it here."

Honey reached up and pulled what looked like a large can with a bunch of holes punched in it out of the nether. She plopped it on the ground and pulled out a bottle of charcoal lighter, some matches, and a small bag of charcoal.

"Where did you get all that?" Brayton asked.

"I've been planning this for a long time. We have to make a really hot fire and throw the tablets in. They're made of pewter I think. They will melt." She was already squeezing the lighter fluid over the coal. A few moments later, a healthy flame was flickering in the brisk air.

He smelled the wolves before he saw them. "Honey, we have company."

She didn't even look up. "I know. They know me."

The group of wolves in human form steadily appeared from three different directions until they were completely surrounded. Honey and the woman kept their attention on the fire. He knew what he had to do.

Pulling up his power, Brayton declared, "You will not harm her or turn her in."

Some of the wolves flinched, but they kept coming. The one Brayton had already identified as the alpha stopped his people a good ten feet from where they were so that a large circle about thirty feet in diameter formed around them.

"Ye are trespassing on our lands."

"Right to roam," Honey said without looking up.

"Honey Smith," he said.

Honey finally looked up and smiled at at the stranger. "Alpha Mac. How's your family?"

He stepped forward and squatted beside her to put his hands out to her fire. Brayton let out a warning growl.

"Aye won't harm her, alpha. Yer power has me trussed up good." He turned his large head to Honey. "Mah folks are well. Dae ye mind tellin' me what you're daein'?"

She picked up the two whole tablets and waved them at him, before dropping them into her now roaring little fire. "Breaking a curse. You might want to get back."

He let out a creative string of cuss words when sparks blasted out of the top of the can. Honey calmly peered inside and tossed in the broken pieces of the other two. More sparks shot out, enough that even Honey scooted away. If he didn't know better, he'd think she'd tossed in box of fireworks.

"You're gonnae set the tree ay fire!" the alpha growled.

"One more."

She pulled a hammer out of the air and slammed it down on the stone she'd stored with the other curses. It split open with a crack as loud as a gun shot. She scooped up the pieces and tossed them into her fire.

A red haze started rising from the flames. Honey popped to her feet and spread out her hands. Brayton blinked twice and was shocked to see white transparent globs about the size of pillows floating up into the branches through the center of a bright column that he realized was coming from Honey.

"What are they?"

"The leftover essence of all the people whose blood was collected to establish the curse."

"That's a lot of people."

"More than I expected," Honey admitted. "I think every time someone was killed, their blood must have strengthened the curse."

"What are ye talkin' about?" the alpha demanded.

"The bits of white floating up," Brayton answered since Honey had that determined, 'I'm concentrating' look on her face. "Don't worry, they're going straight up. I don't think they'll cause any problems."

"Mair ghosts. Like Jay."

Honey shook her head. "No, not like Jay. They are just memories."

"Where hae ye been?" Alpha Mac asked Brayton after a couple of minutes of watching the sparks. Instead of abating, they appeared to be getting stronger and higher, much higher than should be possible from a small charcoal fire. Amazingly, the tree did not catch fire and the sparks did not fly out over the people even though the breeze was brisk. They stayed within the confines of Honey's glowing column all the way up to where the red glow reflected off the bottom of the low-hanging clouds.

"With a..." was the spell woman a friend, an acquaintance? He wasn't sure how to classify her. "... woman."

"She main be powerful. Th' whole world has bin lookin' fur ye two."

"Yes. She is."

"There's a reward fur ye."

"What else is new?"

Brayton heard rather than saw some vehicles skid to a stop on loose gravel somewhere past the tree. Wisps of magic came from somewhere behind him, portals maybe. He pulled up more of his power and released his command, slightly modified, again. "You will not harm or attempt to capture anyone here."

Honey gave him a stomach-melting smile over the flames which were now only equal to the height of the can. A moment later, they were almost gone.

"One last thing," she said, and put her hand out over the can.

The single drop of blood she squeezed out shimmered like a little moon right until it disappeared into the can. Even though it was only one drop, he heard the sizzle, and saw the shadow that blasted out from all sides of the can. Maybe it was his imagination, but even in the dark, everything looked lighter.

Honey let four more drops fall, then dropped her hand and gave him a triumphant grin. "We did it."

"You did."

He opened his arms. She reached to embrace him.

Then she was gone.

"Honey? HONEY!?"

Brayton stood and frantically searched the darkness surrounding the nearly extinguished flames. He noted lots of

186

shapes. A crowd of people had gathered while the fire was burning, but none of them were Honey. His eyes fell on Theodosia on the other side of the can just as her head slumped forward.

He leaped over the can to catch her shoulders before she fell backwards. "What's wrong? Are you okay?"

"I see – a room," she whispered.

"Where?"

"Honey is ... on a bed. There is something on her head... a band...powerful, and there's red on her arm. She looks pale."

"Do you know where it is? Do you see anything that might tell me?"

"White walls. A woman. A bowl of red liquid."

"Bluid?" Alpha Mac asked.

"A big man in the doorway. He is angry," Theodosia continued as if Mac hadn't said anything. "They are arguing."

"What are they saying?" Brayton begged.

Theodosia responded, but in a deeper voice that was not quite her own, "You are taking too much."

She then looked over her shoulder and said in a higher pitch. "She's half wolf. She will survive."

Theodosia looked forward again and raised her head. Her eyes had gone completely white. "I need her alive!" she said in the deeper voice.

Theodosia put her hands on her hips and said in the female voice. "I acquired the artifacts. I brought her here. I subdued her. I've done all the work. All you've done is moan and complain. You can have her after I'm done with her. If you're so worried, I suggest you get some blood to replace what I'm taking because I'm going to need it all to make it

187

worth my while. Ah ah ah. I told you not to cross that line. Freeze charm. Now you get to stand there and watch while I finish."

Theodosia's head sagged forward. A moment later, she took a deep breath and raised her head. Her eyes were back to normal except for the shine.

"Is that happening now?" Brayton asked, he didn't recognize his own voice.

"Nae," Alpha Mac said. "It takes a while tae drain a body like 'at." He reached forward and took Theodosia's pale hands and asked in a gentle voice. "Can ye describe the man? Was he a wolf or a witch?"

"Wolf. The woman was a witch. She was middle-aged. He was younger. Short brown hair. Nice looking, but his eyes were cold. He had big fists."

That could be anyone.

"Did ye see any rings, necklaces, scars, anything 'at might help us identify them folk?" Alpha Mac asked.

Theodosia closed her eyes. Brayton couldn't breath. Someone had Honey. Maybe he could pull her to him the way she always pulled him to her. It was easy to send his clothes to the nether when he transformed, but he'd never managed to send anything the way she could. Maybe now was the time.

Theodosia mentioned a ring and a necklace and a wide bracelet the man was wearing but none of it was going to help in time.

"Could ye portal tae them?" Alpha Mac asked.

"I am not a portal maker," Theodosia said.

"Ah, but we hae portal charms."

Alpha Mac gestured to a woman dressed in black standing outside of the circle formed by his pack. She stepped forward. He spoke to her, then offered Theodosia the small item the woman had, somewhat reluctantly, Brayton thought, handed to him.

"Do you know how to use it?" Brayton asked while Theodosia stared at the shell laying in her palm.

"Yes." She wrapped her fingers around the charm. "But I'm not sure what good I'll do myself."

"It will stay open for ten seconds or until you go through," Brayton said. "I'll go through first."

"Ten seconds?" Theodosia commented, studying the charm again. "Back in my day it was instantaneous and only the person or persons holding the charm could go."

"I'm going tae," Alpha Mac declared. "Dean, Callen, you're wi' me."

"Oh nae, wolfie boy, dinnae think you're gonnae take mah charm 'en have all th' fun," the woman in black said. She looked over her shoulder at another woman all in black except for the bright red bush on her head. "Come on, Esme."

Theodosia closed her eyes. "I'm picturing the room."

Brayton smelled the portal magic, but couldn't see it in the dark until he turned on his magic vision. The portal had opened up right on top of the now barely-glowing fire. Without hesitation, he jumped.

A moment later, he stumbled into a room so bright, he couldn't see anything. Knowing there would be someone right behind him, he let himself go forward another step. After another moment, his eyes had adjusted enough to see a dark form leaning over something on a table.

"STOP!"

The face of the form twisted toward him and he registered the woman's smirk even as the pointy object in her hand slammed into Honey's chest.

"NO! HONEY!"

He leaped to Honey's side and put his hands over the hole in her chest, but he knew if the knife had pierced her heart, it was useless. Where was the knife? He looked up just long enough to see it disappearing into the wall along with the awful, murdering woman. A weird feeling washed over him and his vision flashed red. Shaking his head to rid himself of the sensation, he turned his attention back to Honey's pale face.

"Honey come on, wake up. You need to freeze yourself. You need to stop the bleeding."

The metal band on her head pulsed evilly. Not only had they stabbed her, they'd spelled her too. Brayton risked removing one hand from Honey's chest to rip the nasty thing off and throw it across the room. The metal didn't like that. A bright light blasted from the object. He caught a whiff of burning hair, but barely felt any heat, thanks to Honey's protection charms, he was sure.

"Here. Let me see. I can help. I'm a healer," a soft voice said from across the table. Pale, feminine hands tried to lift his away.

He gave in when a stronger, larger, hairier pair joined in. He knew he wasn't helping Honey. It was the nightmare at the club all over again except this time he was sober and now he knew what she meant to him.

She was too pale. Was she even breathing? He pushed away from whoever held him so he could talk directly in Honey's ear and touch her soft curls. "Honey, hang on. Don't leave me. You broke the curse. You have to live so you can do all those things you wanted to do."

She *was* breathing, very rapidly, as if she couldn't get enough air.

Then she wasn't.

"Come on Honey. Breathe!"

The door across the room slammed open. Brayton recognized the wolf's smell before he recognized the face.

The two wolves alpha Mac had brought with him stepped forward to intercept the intruder but Deacon waved them away with a pulse of alpha power, then raised his hand. It took a moment for Brayton to realize what Deacon was pointing at him.

"You're going to shoot me?"

"Only if you don't get away from my mate."

"*Your* mate?"

Not only had Deacon stole his father's and his brother's alpha powers, now he was trying to steal a mate too?

Frustration, anger, a need to protect – too many emotions to identify flushed through Brayton. He rose to his feet. Red pulsed again, and the glow from the measly bit of protection magic around Deacon's neck and whatever was on Deacon's wrist vanished. Brayton didn't give any commands, he simply visualized what he wanted to happen and Deacon complied. Like a new leaf under a scorching desert sun, Deacon withered under Brayton's stare, dropping the gun, and then dropping to his knees, and finally curling into a ball so that his head was on the floor.

A woman's voice in his ear brought Brayton back to himself. "There's nothing more I can do. She's gone."

"No. She can't be gone. Did you seal up the wound?"

"Yes, but…"

Brayton turned his attention on the other woman. "I need a portal."

He could tell the other witch didn't want to give away another of her precious portals, but with his powers he didn't give her much of choice. He scooped up Honey and visualized where he wanted to be.

"Can I go?" Theodosia asked.

"Yes, and the healer. Go."

23

BRAYTON – DECEMBER 13 – INDIANA

"We've got her stabilized. There's nothing more to do but wait. You should get some rest," Dr. Ziga said, pulling the gloves off his hands.

"I'll stay here."

"You sure? I can hear your stomach. I know Honey wouldn't want you to starve yourself for her sake."

"What if someone else tries to snatch her while I'm gone? I was just lucky Theodosia saw where she went." Brayton released a shaky sigh and swiped at the tear that had escaped his eye.

"How about Chinese? They deliver," Dr. Ziga said cheerily.

"I don't have money."

"I'll add it to the bill," Dr. Ziga said.

"Ah love Chinese," the Enforcer healer spoke for the first time since telling Dr. Ziga how she'd treated Honey.

"What is Chinese? Is it good?" Theodosia asked from the corner of the room. Brayton had all but forgotten she was there.

"Very," Dr. Ziga smiled at her. "I'm sorry, I didn't catch your name."

"Theodosia Wixx," she curtsied. "I am a distant cousin of Honey's. She rescued me from a curse I was trapped in for over 200 years."

"Really? Then this must be quite new to you?" He indicated the room with a wave of his hand.

"Yes," she agreed looking around the room. "I have much to learn."

"Well, Chinese food is a great place to start. I'll get all the best dishes so you can try them."

"I'd like some too," the nurse said, "since you're buying."

"Always the kidder, Darlene."

Dr. Ziga slid to the door so smoothly, it looked like he was floating. He abruptly halted though when he opened the door.

"What is her status?" a gruff voice demanded from the hallway.

Dr. Ziga slipped through the door and closed it most of the way behind him, leaving a small crack through which everyone in the room could still hear the conversation.

"Who are you?"

"Agent Emmanuel Jones. I'm here to take Honey Smith into custody."

"I will need to see more than a badge before I disclose anything about my patient."

The door clicked shut.

Brayton's chest squeezed. How had the enforcers already found them? What should he do? What could he do? Honey was still unconscious and hooked up to a bag of blood. He couldn't move her.

"Did you tell them where we were?" Brayton asked the healer.

She lifted up her wrist to show a flat black band with a square watch face. "Tracker. It's fur the best. Ye cannae keep runnin'. Besides th' curse is broken noo. She will be safe."

"Assuming people believe it."

"She's tay injured tae be taken intae custody right noo anyway. Ah ken ye wolves heal fast, but she's lost a lot ay bluid."

He didn't need the reminder. "Thank you for helping her. I don't know what I would do if I lost her."

He'd almost lost her, again. He might still lose her. He sat down and buried his face into Honey's shoulder and hugged her while the tears he could no longer contain dampened her blanket. Somewhere in the room someone was talking but it wasn't until the end of the conversation that he realized it was the healer talking to her watch.

"Yes sir. Nae sir, twelve hours at least. Yes sir." She tapped her watch and lowered her arm when she realized Brayton was watching. "Ah get tae stay with ye overnight."

"What do you call those boxes with wheels? They almost look like carriages but there are no horses." Theodosia said from the window.

"Where?" the healer asked, moving to peer over Theodosia's shoulder.

"There, that white box with the big letters on the side. People are getting out."

"That is a van, a news van," the healer said, shooting a glance in Brayton's direction before grabbing the drapes and tugging them closed. "Best tae get away from the windae."

195

"There's a wolf right under the window," Theodosia whispered. "I can feel him."

The healer glanced again at Brayton. "Can ye dae something about that, Mr. Alpha?"

He already was. He pulled up his power and sent out a strong compulsion to back off and stay away.

"Woah, I didn't mean me," the healer said.

Both she and Theodosia backed into the nearest wall and looked like they were trying to push themselves into it.

"Sorry."

Brayton pulled back his power then focused it on the parking lot.

The door burst open. A wolf dressed as an enforcer with his taser ready stepped inside. "What was that?"

"Go back to your post and guard the door," Brayton commanded. "Don't let anyone inside but Dr. Ziga and the nurses."

The big wolf immediately ducked his head and backed out, although from the look on his face he wasn't happy about it.

"Geez," the healer said. "Ah would nae want tae be part of yer pack if ye ever got ragin'. Are all wolves in th' states as strong as ye?"

"No."

"More vans just parked in the yard," Theodosia said, peering behind the edge of the drapes. "They're black."

The healer pulled back the drapes to look herself. "More enforcers ah bet. They'll be settin' up a perimeter."

"What is that?" Theodosia asked. "It looks almost like a big gun."

"It is a big gun. Sheet, gie down."

Brayton covered Honey with his body expecting an immediate boom. Nothing happened. He turned his head to see the healer peering up over the bottom of the window. "What do you see?"

"A second gun. People in black spreading out."

"They aren't enforcers?"

"No."

"I feel wolves," Theodosia said just as the Enforcer outside the door yelled, "Freeze".

There was an idea. Brayton pulled up his power again then released it all around with the same command.

"Tell me you have a portal," he whispered toward the healer, willing his power to release her and Theodosia at the same time.

She nodded, her eyes wide.

"Give it to me."

"She really shouldn't be moved."

"We don't have a choice. Hurry before someone else comes."

The healer nodded in agreement and stood. "You carry her. I'll bring the stands so we can keep her fluids going. Theodosia, grab that other bag of liquid there. We should be safe at headquarters."

"No," Brayton said. "Someone leaked she was here and I'm certain it wasn't Dr. Ziga's people. I know a place where absolutely no one will harm her."

"I can't let you…" the healer began.

"Give me the portal," Brayton demanded with all his power, "then freeze."

197

He swiped the metallic charm with a big 'P' etched in the center from the woman's outstretched hand then set the empty bag of saline on Honey's stomach.

"Theodosia, you bring the stands."

"Shouldn't we take her with us?" Theodosia asked while Brayton unhooked Honey from everything but the IV bag.

"I would," he replied, "but I don't know how many trackers she has. I don't want anyone to follow us."

As carefully as he could, he scooped up Honey and hugged her to his chest. They'd cleaned her up, but her limp body still smelled like blood. He blinked to clear his eyes of the gathering moisture then pictured his destination.

"Go."

24

HONEY – DECEMBER 14 – SOMEPLACE WARM

She was warm, pleasantly so. There was no fire, not even the tiniest stench of it. She did smell sulfur though. The smell was familiar, but why? Where had she smelled that before? She wasn't in the necklace. There were too many distant bird calls and creaking branches and the faint voices of people. She tried a deeper breath and wasn't surprised that her lungs hurt. Why? A fire maybe, but, no, this was more of a bruise pain. She sniffed again. No smoke, but there was a familiar smell – a smell that made her stomach quiver – the scent of someone who hadn't been there until days after the fire.

She opened her eyes. The light coming in through the window was dim, but there was enough to see a messy head of dirty-blond hair resting on the side of her bed. Seeing him there at her side made something in her belly give a little flip. She reached over and slipped her fingers into his soft hair.

"Brayton?"

Her voice came out as more of a whisper than she'd intended, but it was enough. Brayton lifted his head and blinked at her blearily, then was suddenly smiling so bright, the three stars hiding on his forehead flashed at her.

"Honey. Honey, you're awake! Oh my gosh, you're awake. You came back. I was afraid..."

He kissed her cheek, then flung himself across her chest to give her a sideways hug. She tried to hug him back but the angle was awkward and he had one of her arms pinned down.

"Brayton, it's okay. I'm here. I'm not going anywhere." She patted his shoulder with her free hand. Why was he so upset? She remembered getting all the pieces of the curse and going to Scotland and lighting the fire, but after that, things got blurry.

"What happened? Didn't it work? Didn't I break the curse?" she squeezed out.

Brayton lifted his head to look at her. His blond stubble and the shadows under his eyes made him look much older than his nineteen years, but it was the tears on his eyelashes that made her heart stutter.

"You did, then you almost died, not from the curse, though. It was from some greedy witch and Deacon."

"Deacon?" Her voice still wouldn't work properly.

"You need water. Here."

He raised her into a sitting position with one arm and stuffed a couple of pillows behind her before handing her a plastic cup half-full of water. She couldn't remember water ever tasting so good.

"Deacon?" she asked again after she'd downed contents of the cup.

"Yep. He decided stealing his brother's and his dad's powers was not enough. He wanted you as his Luna. He made a deal with the witch. He provided a location and security and she came up with the magic to snatch you. In return, she got some of your blood and he got the rest of you, theoretically alive, but the witch got greedy or maybe she never intended to

200

share. She was draining your arm of blood, then when I showed up, she stabbed your chest and ran."

"Who was the witch?"

"I don't know and I don't care. She won't bother you again."

"She's dead?"

He nodded, his look fierce. Had he killed her?

"What happened?" she asked gently.

"Portal failure. She got stuck in the wall along with a bowl of your blood when she tried to run."

"That can happen?!"

"Apparently. It's extremely rare though." He sighed and laid his head on her bed so it was also resting on her shoulder.

"Where are we?"

It was clearly a bedroom, sparsely decorated like a hotel room, but it didn't feel or smell like a hotel. In fact, she sniffed, it smelled of cement dust, new wood, and fresh paint, like it was brand new.

"Zavier's"

"I don't recognize this building."

"It's one of the new cabins they're building on the property. Zavier thought it would be easier to keep our presence a secret if as few people as possible knew you were here, so he put us in one that they're still finishing up. It has heat and water and electricity though."

"Is everything okay?" A female voice asked from the doorway. "Oh, you are awake! I am glad."

Honey recognized the woman but couldn't remember her name. She looked like she'd just stepped out of a historical movie. "I'm sorry, I don't..."

The woman curtsied. "Theodosia Wixx. You rescued me from a curse. I'm not surprised you don't remember."

"Sorry. I remember now," and she did. "I imagine things are really different from when you were born."

"Some are, some are not," Theodosia agreed. "The television is interesting. When you are better, you can give me a proper tour."

"I'd love to!" Honey said and meant it with all her heart. "How long was I out?"

"One day and some," Brayton replied. "It's about 11 pm, local time. How do you feel?"

"Fine," she shrugged and flinched when something twinged painfully in the center of her chest. "A little sore," she admitted.

"Hungry?"

Her stomach responded for her.

Brayton chuckled. "Yep. Theodosia, why don't you stay with her while I make her some food."

"I can do it."

"Please. One of us should stay with her and I don't want the cabin to burn down."

"Ouch!" Honey interjected.

He rolled his eyes. "She tried to light a fire in the stove, Honey. It's a gas stove."

"Well, excuse me for never seeing one before!" Theodosia huffed.

"And she put a whole loaf of bread in the microwave."

"I thought it was a breadbox."

"Did she turn it on?" Honey asked curiously.

"Yes!" He was grinning. His white teeth glinted in the starlight coming in through the window. "We're just lucky it had a plastic closure instead of a metal tie."

"There was an 'on' button. I thought it meant I had to turn it on."

"I can see that," Honey said politely, then asked the question she really needed to know. "Is the toilet functional?"

"Yes. Do you need to go?"

Honey gave Brayton a 'you've got to be kidding me' look.

"Right. Here, let me help you."

"No," Theodosia stepped forward. "You fix her food. I will help her."

"She's heavier than she looks."

"Thanks!" Honey huffed.

"I have much experience tending to the invalid. Go," Theodosia ordered sternly.

Honey braced herself, then pulled her covers back. The air was definitely cooler, but not as bad as it could have been. To her surprise, she was wearing a hospital gown. She sniffed at the edges of it. Dr. Ziga? Was he here too or had she been there? What else had happened while she was out?

"Can you walk?" Theodosia asked.

"Probably." Honey twisted so her feet were on the floor, then let Theodosia help her up. The world spun.

"Just take it slow," her cousin said.

"Who were the invalids you tended?" Honey asked against Theodosia's shoulder while she waited for the light-headed feeling to pass. She wondered when her cousin had last bathed herself or her clothes. She didn't smell bad, but there was definitely some sweat and woodsmoke soaked into the

203

fibers of her woolen dress, some of it likely hundreds of years old.

"My aunt was a healer. I served as her assistant even though I am not a healer myself."

"You were the muscle?"

"Indeed."

Honey took a deep breath and lifted her head. The first few steps were wobbly, but with Theodosia's steady support, she made it across the room and to the bathroom just outside the door.

"I've got it from here."

"Are you sure?" Theodosia asked doubtfully.

"Yeah. In fact, I think I'll take a shower. I always feel better after one of them. Have you taken one before?"

"No."

"You'll like it, assuming the hot water is working. I'll test it first."

The hot water *was* working. There was even a bar of soap, but no towels or shampoo. Honey pulled a bag of clothes from the nether and used a shirt to dry off, then dressed in the last of her fresh clothes. She desperately needed to do some laundry.

The lovely fragrance of freshly cooked bacon greeted her when she stepped out the door of the centrally located bathroom between the two bedrooms. Across the combined living, dining, and kitchen area Brayton lifted a plate in her direction piled with not just bacon, but eggs and toast too.

She swallowed. "I didn't know you could cook."

"There's a lot you don't know about me."

"Really?"

He wiggled his eyebrows and pulled out a chair for her at the small table.

"Do you want to sit at the table or eat in the bed?" Theodosia asked. Honey hadn't even noticed her waiting near the bathroom door.

"I can sit."

Theodosia nodded and indicated Honey should go before her. "You wolves really do heal quickly."

"She's a fast healer," Brayton said, pushing her chair in for her, then kissing her on top of the head.

It was sweet. She'd never thought of him as sweet before.

"Do the lights not work," she asked, waving her fork at the candle in the center of the table. They had in the bathroom.

"They do, but we're trying not to bring too much attention to ourselves," Brayton explained.

"I'm sure the pack knows someone is here."

"Yes. Zavier told them a witch friend of yours was staying here temporarily."

"It wouldn't be the first time," Honey nodded right before she shoved a big bite of scrambled eggs into her mouth. "Mmm!" There was cheese.

The knock on the door was firm, yet polite.

"Speak of the devil," Brayton nodded toward the door.

Theodosia smoothly maneuvered around the table and opened it a crack to look out before finally opening it all the way and giving a little curtsy.

"Good evening, Alpha Zavier."

"Good evening, Miss Wixx, I see my cousin is awake. May I come in?"

"Please."

Honey shot a questioning look at Brayton, but he was busy smirking at her cousins.

"Why are you two being so formal?" Honey asked.

"I'm not being formal. I'm being polite," Zavier said, stepping inside.

"And how did you know I was awake?"

"Why else would someone be cooking bacon at this hour?" His long legs quickly covered the short space to the table and a moment later he was crouched beside her with his arms around her and his head on her shoulder. "It's so good to see you again, little cousin."

She put her fork down and hugged him back. "How is everyone? How big is your pack now?"

He released her and sat in the other chair at the table. "Big and getting bigger. There were over forty the last time I bothered to count."

"Did you build your hotel yet?"

"Resort," he corrected. "The plans are drawn. I'm still working on the funding. If all goes well, we will break ground when the weather warms up in the spring."

"How's your son?"

"He's a little terror. Spoiled rotten by everyone but me, of course."

"And his mother?"

"She's going to college and majoring in women's studies."

"Really?" It made sense. Maya had grown up in a culture where women were expected to become wives and mothers and nothing else. She'd become the youngest bride of a man

206

with several wives when she was sixteen but had eventually run away. "Good for her."

"Walter says she's seeing someone."

"Oh, I'm sorry."

"It's okay," her cousin said with a little smile. "She's getting on with her life. That's the whole point of this pack."

"Still," Honey squeezed the hand that was resting on the table. "She couldn't do better than you for a husband."

He leaned forward and kissed her temple. "You're sweet, Honey. Get it?"

She rolled her eyes. "Har. Har."

"Anyway," he put both palms down on the table. "I think we should let your respective parents know where you are. I've been thinking of inviting them here anyway to discuss the resort plans since they've both expressed an interest in investing. It would be a good excuse for them to come here."

"It's too obvious," Honey argued. "People know I'm back. They know I had to go somewhere. They'll be watching them."

Zavier shrugged. "Who's to say you haven't gone back to where you were before? I contact Uncle Rory and your parents," he nodded to Brayton, "often enough it won't be odd. Besides, you haven't even met your little brother, Honey, and he's already a year old."

"Brother?" Brayton asked.

"Alpha Silver is my biological father," Honey explained. "It was in my dad's letter. Bio-dad didn't know about me until after he met me."

Brayton gaped at her for a moment, then asked, "Can I read the letter?"

207

"Sure."

He gently squeezed her hand and gave a her soft, tummy-melting smile before turning his attention to Zavier.

"Why have you been in contact with my parents?"

"Your dad is your power of attorney and your mom makes good suggestions. Besides, being involved in something helps her cope, I think."

"Cope with what?"

"Losing the baby. Losing you."

"She really was pregnant?"

"Yeah. She lost it shortly after you disappeared. It's common in the first trimester."

Brayton looked calm, but Honey could feel his grief and tension. She reached over and squeezed his fist. "I think it's a good idea, Zavier. Go ahead and invite them. Maybe give me a few days to recover."

"Sure. Anything for my favorite cousin."

25

BRAYTON - DECEMBER 20 - YELLOWSTONE

The door opened and Theo slipped inside. She looked like any other twenty-something female now that she was wearing modern clothes. "They are here."

"Did they see you?" Honey asked.

"If they did, it was not well. I stayed in the shadows near the big cabin."

He had to know. "Was my mother there?"

"I believe so. I could not hear much from where I was standing, but there was a woman with hair like yours who looked around like she was searching for someone and she was standing next to an alpha who looked like you."

Brayton's stomach clenched. Had Mom managed to convert Dad to her way of thinking?

"There was an older man and woman standing with them."

"Probably my grandparents."

"He noticed me. He looked me right in the eye."

"Were you upwind? He might have smelled my scent on you."

"I do not know. I do not see that it mattered. I was next to the building."

"Maybe he smelled the gingerbread," Honey said, plopping another hot tray of them on the counter.

They did smell good. Brayton would be surprised if his grandfather didn't smell the cookies. Honey had been baking all morning. He understood. After five days of hunkering in the cabin not only to avoid the pack, but the drones that had appeared after Zavier had sent the invite, he was suffering from a bad case of cabin fever too.

"How long do you think it will be before Zavier brings them by?" Honey asked.

"Thirty minutes? An hour? Depends if they want the full tour of the site now or later. Or maybe now," he said when someone knocked on the door.

Theo looked through the peephole, then opened the door a crack. "Alpha Zavier, what brings you to my door?"

"Miss Theo, this is Alpha Silver, Luna Tanya, and their son Mathias. We have more visitors than I was expecting. I was wondering if they could use your spare bedroom tonight."

That was the first time Brayton had heard Zavier call Theodosia by her first name, and he'd used the shortened form, no less. Was he doing it at her request or because people might be listening in? Theo glanced behind her, clearly wondering about the bedroom situation. There were only two bedrooms and they were already taken, but it was a good excuse for bringing Alpha Silver here. Brayton shrugged and nodded. Theodosia opened the door. Honey stood in the shadow of the door and greeted each person that entered with her finger over her lips and a charmed hair band.

"What is this for?" Zavier asked as soon as the door was shut.

"Protection and I've added a muffling spell so if anyone is trying to listen in magically, they shouldn't be able to understand what we're saying."

"Honey!" Alpha Silver pulled her into a tight hug. He'd put the band on without hesitation.

Honey made a face when he planted a hard kiss on the top of her head. "Dad."

"Da da da da da da," the dark-headed baby in his mother's arms added.

Alpha Silver released Honey and spun around to take the boy and present him to Honey. "This is your brother. Mathias, this is your amazing big sister. Can you say Hon-ey?"

The boy blinked his big brown eyes at her for a moment, then held his hands out toward her. "E e e."

A brilliant smile spread across Honey's face. She handed her bowl of hairbands off to Theo, then lifted the little boy out of Alpha Silver's arms.

"I've been wanting to meet you for so long."

Mathias closed and opened his fists like he wanted something. "E e e."

"What does that mean?"

"He wants a hug," Luna Silver said, stepping around her husband.

Honey complied. The boy did rest his head against her for a moment, but then he launched himself up, grabbed a fist full of hair on either side of her face, and pulled. Before Honey could get lose, he planted a big kiss on her forehead where the three stars could still be faintly seen.

211

"Mine."

The other adults laughed. Brayton didn't. He plucked the kid out of Honey's hands and turned him around so they could speak man-to-baby. "You are too young for her, plus, she's your sister. She's mine."

"Mine mine mine."

Honey shook her head and took the baby back. "Brayton, he doesn't understand." She looked the baby in the eye. "I can't be yours but," she placed a gentle, yet lingering kiss on the baby's forehead.

"Mine," he insisted when she pulled back.

She shook her head and tickled him. "Silly."

"E stop. E stop!"

"He doesn't like to be tickled," his mom said, taking him back.

"Sorry."

The baby glared. Honey winced, then rubbed her head. "I said sorry."

"Not eared. Not eared!"

"Why is he saying that?" Brayton asked.

Alpha Silver shook his head. "I don't know."

"*I told him I didn't know he was weird about being tickled,*" Honey sent. "*I guess babies can understand telepathic messages.*"

"Better hope he doesn't figure out how to send them back," Brayton said out loud, earning some confused looks.

"*Too late.*"

Alpha Silver stuck his hand out toward Theo. "I don't think we've met. I'm Alpha Silver, Honey's dad."

"Rory," Tanya said with a warning in her tone.

He missed Theodosia's curtsy because he'd already turned his head to speak to his wife. "It doesn't matter now. She broke the curse."

"Yeah, but that doesn't mean you can go around telling people you fathered a hybrid. It might not bother *you* if people know but think how cruel the other kids will be to Mathias when he starts school. Plus, it could affect our pack businesses and…"

"Fine," he looked back at Theodosia and wiggled his hand. "I'm Honey's Uncle."

Theodosia cautiously put her palm against his. "I am Theodosia, Theo for short. I'm a distant cousin of Honey's, on her mother's side."

"You're a witch," he said, wrapping his other hand around hers while continuing to his vigorous shaking.

"Yes."

"That's super. I'm glad she's getting to know both sides of her family. Is that where she's been hiding out, with you?"

"No."

"Da..Uncle Rory, let her go." Honey grabbed Alpha Silver's and Theo's wrists and pulled them apart. "She's from the 1700's. They curtsied and bowed back then. She's not used to shaking hands."

"The 1700's? Really?" Tanya said with interest. "I'm kind of a history buff. Well, not really. I like historical novels, but I always wonder how accurate they are. Wait. How did you get here? Can witches time travel?"

"Alpha Zavier, are you in there?" a familiar voice called from outside. "I was wondering if we could get some coffee before the tour."

Brayton's stomach tightened at the sound of Grandpa's voice. Was Grandpa still on Honey's side? He took Honey's hand and pulled her away from the door both so they couldn't be seen from outside when the door opened and so he'd have room to defend her if he had to. Zavier wiggled his eyebrows at them, then opened the door with a flourish. "Come on in Alpha Braxton and family."

This time it was Theo with her finger over her lips and the bowl of head bands.

"Bra…"

Brayton cut his mom's approach off with a firm shake of his head and a shot of alpha power to stop her feet, then pointed at the bowl. He and Honey moved further back so everyone could fit. The cabin was spacious when there were only three people in it, but with eleven, five and a baby of which were alphas, it was close to claustrophobic. Wisely, the alphas left all the betas outside.

Zavier shut the door and turned to grin and rub his hands together. "I'll have Beta Ruth make a fresh pot of coffee and you can help yourself to some cookies. After you put on the handy anti-listening charms Honey made," he waved his hair-banded wrist around, "you can commence the grilling."

That was all the encouragement Brayton's mother needed to finally slip the yellow band she'd been holding suspiciously onto her wrist. A moment later Brayton's arms were pinned to his sides in an enthusiastic hug.

"Brayton. I've missed you so much. Where have you been?"

"With my mate."

214

Before he could properly gage her reaction, his dad was pulling him into a more comfortable hug, one where he could use his arms to hug back. "Brayton, son. It's good to see you again."

"Dad."

"My turn," Grandpa said, right before he not only squeezed Brayton like a lemon but gave him a vigorous noogie.

"Grandpa!"

"Braxton, behave," Grandma said, then pulled Brayton into the gentlest hug of all. While she was still hugging him, she stretched out a hand to Honey. "And how are you my dear."

"I'm good."

His grandmother released him, then pulled a reluctant Honey into her arms. "I'm glad." She released Honey, then faced them both with her hands on her hips. "Now explain yourselves. Where were you and how many people do you have in your pack, Alpha Brayton?"

26

HONEY – DECEMBER 20 – YELLOWSTONE

Honey sipped at the tea she'd opted to drink instead of the pitch-black liquid Beta Ruth called coffee. Everyone else was drinking it, including Theo, but she noticed a generous use of sugar and cream going on, even by Alpha Brandon. Alpha Braxton, of course, was drinking it straight, and smiling in pleasure, or pain. She truly couldn't tell. At least the cookies tasted good.

Her baby brother certainly liked them based on his verbal and telepathic begging followed by a severe scolding when she didn't acquiesce to his demands. He didn't appreciate her sitting across the doorway and preventing him from exploring the other half of the cabin while the big people were distracted either. Were all babies so opinionated and bossy and sly? She had a feeling he either didn't talk to his parents telepathically or they couldn't yet hear him, because they were treating him like he was the sweetest little guy in the world when he clearly wasn't.

"And then we came here," Brayton finished. He was a little lower than everyone one else since he was sitting on the coffee table and they were on the couch or the dining room chairs. It looked like he was giving a lecture in one of those liberal arts classes where everyone sat around in a circle, not that she'd taken one yet.

"What are your plans next," Brayton's dad asked.

"He has to finish school," his mom interrupted.

"Lynn, he has his own pack now, even if it is a very small one. He's an adult. He can make his own decisions. As your father, though," Alpha Brandon turned to Brayton, "I would advise finishing. We will still pay your tuition, of course, and Honey's if Lynn can't get the scholarship reinstated."

He winked at Honey when she looked up at him in surprise.

"There's no way that's going to happen, not with her criminal record. She's wanted for theft, kidnapping, attempted murder, murder, destruction of private property, need I go on?" Lynn protested.

"What?" Honey and Brayton said at the same time.

"Did you or did you not steal from and blow up a library in Chicago?" Lynn challenged.

"I did not."

"Then why was your DNA all over it?"

"Was it my DNA they detected? I thought it was my blood or my essence."

"Were you there?" Alpha Brandon asked.

"Yes, but I didn't set off a bomb or steal anything that belonged to the library. I was retrieving a collection that the library had stolen from someone else."

"That young witch whose magical aunt turned out to be a serial killer?" Brayton's grandfather asked.

"Yes. The library confiscated everything in the house to 'protect it'," she said with air quotes, "but they weren't

217

planning on returning it. They were cataloging it to put on their shelves. It wasn't right so I fixed it."

"That collection was dangerous," Lynn scolded. "It shouldn't be loose in public."

"It was no more dangerous than what other witches collect and it was never loose. A person couldn't just walk off the street and take it. That stuff was created or collected by her family for centuries. It was her heritage. For them to steal it would be like them taking your pack lands away."

"What about the bomb?" Alpha Brandon asked. "Where did that come from?"

"I don't know. Someone found a way to portal it at me using my blood. I barely escaped. I just happened to be in the library when they did it."

"What about that old human in Australia?" Lynn demanded.

"What old human?"

"What was his name?" she frowned at Alpha Brandon. "It reminded me of mayonnaise."

"Helman?"

"Arthur Helman?" Honey asked.

"Yes. That's it."

"What about him?"

"Why did you kill him?"

Her stomach gave an unpleasant lurch. "He's dead? When? How?"

"You didn't know?" Alpha Brandon interrupted before Lynn could answer.

"No. I stayed with him for a little while as his caretaker, but I didn't kill him, nor did I ever consider it. He was a nice man. He took me in and protected me."

Poor Mr. Helman. She hoped he hadn't died because he'd helped her.

"What about the bank robberies?"

"What bank robberies?"

Lynn opened her mouth to reply but Honey cut her off. "You know what, never mind. I haven't been in a bank for well over a year, and even then I didn't rob it."

"It's pretty clear it was just someone trying to make it look like it was you," her bio-dad said comfortingly. "Only the hard-core Honey-haters continue to insist it was you. Oh," he winced. "I didn't mean you Lynn."

"Then how did she support herself?" Lynn sniffed. "She didn't have that much money."

Honey pulled her tent out of the nether. "I had a couple of thousand on gift cards and I didn't need a lot. I camped, mostly for free, and ate a lot of peanut butter sandwiches."

Brayton abruptly left his table to sit behind her on the floor and wrap himself around her.

"*What's wrong?*" she sent.

He kissed her ear, then whispered, "I don't like to think of you being alone like that."

Alpha Brayton rubbed his chin. "I bet we can get most of the charges dropped with the proper representation, and if the repeal goes through, as it should, you should be free to attend classes.

"Repeal?" Honey asked.

"Of the hybrid law. Your friend Nathan and his alpha got an amendment passed that if the curse was broken, the law would be repealed. The challenge is proving it."

"Wow." That's all she could say. Brayton hugged her closer when the tears started to fall.

"No cry. No cry," her little brother said, hugging her from the side. He climbed into her lap, supposedly for a better angle, but she knew he was just trying to crawl over her, the sneaky little devil.

Wait a second. How was he transmitting without being in his wolf form?

"Well," Lynn said, "if all the charges are dropped and the law repealed, I might be able to get her scholarship reinstated, at least partially." She tapped her chin thoughtfully. "I could sell it as a progressive move seeing as how integration is a stated goal of the college. We might even be able to use it for publicity, if Honey's popularity flips around, that is. If I'm going to do that though, Brayton has to rejoin the pack."

"Mom, it's not that simple. Honey is not a normal Luna and I…"

Lynn let out an amused huff. "Truer words were never spoken, but you can't just be a pack of two. That's never going to work. The pack needs you. Your father and I need you and we miss you. I miss you. You're my baby boy, my only child."

Brayton tensed behind her. "Mom, you kidnapped me and let your brother torture me."

"He only held you in a cell and talked to you. That's not torture."

Honey put an open palm on Brayton's chest and willed him to be calm, not because she didn't think Lynn didn't deserve to be chastised, but because he didn't deserve to be angered again.

Brayton kissed the top of her head, then said in stern, yet calm voice, "He poisoned my food, did he mention that? He was trying to brainwash me and find out things about Honey that he could use to kill her."

"She was a wanted criminal at the time. She still is."

"But you can't do anything about it, not here," Brayton said firmly, pulling Honey even tighter to his chest. "The protection on this place will kick you out and I will do everything in my power to protect her. I love her Mom. She is my family and my pack now. I go where she goes."

His father reached over and took his wife's hand. "Lynn, we can discuss this later. It's enough to know he's alive and well for now and has a safe place to stay?" He directed his question at Zavier.

"Yep, my pack is Honey's pack, literally."

Honey rolled her eyes. She still couldn't believe he'd named his pack the Honey pack.

"They can stay here as long as needed," Zavier continued. "And don't worry about Brayton's sanity, Lynn. Like Brayton said, Honey is not like other Lunas. Her powers will ensure he's fine. Plus, as a Celestial Luna, she is above all alphas, even her mate. Alphas know this. We can feel it. Your husband can't accept her into his pack, but she can accept him as one of hers."

"Why would anyone want to join her? She's a hybrid and a troublemaker." Lynn snapped.

"Why do wolves feel the need to howl at the moon, Lynn? I can't explain it, I just know it was the right thing to do. Plus, the legends are true. She rewards those who pledge to her. She boosted my ability to read people, and I can see how difficult all this has been for you. You did the right thing taking Honey in. Brayton's life is not ruined, it will just be different from what you expected, fuller even. You were only trying to protect him, he knows that, but Honey was never the enemy."

Lynn sighed and ducked her head. Her whispered, "I know," was so faint, Honey wasn't sure she'd heard it right, but she must have because Brayton abruptly left her to join his dad in comforting his mom.

Bio-dad's phone dinged. He ignored it until it dinged three more times then started ringing. "I better take this…oh," he said, once he'd looked at the screen. "You guys are going to want to see this."

He set his phone on the coffee table. Honey didn't bother getting up since she doubted she'd be able to see with everyone else crowding around the small screen. Plus, her little brother was not-so-innocently watching for his opportunity to slip by while pretending to be completely absorbed with chewing on a block by the end of the couch. She could hear the phone just fine anyway.

"Earlier this morning, shortly after a visit by renowned seer Salina Chanel, the Super Council ruled that unless future evidence suggests otherwise, the hybrid law will no longer be enforced. This means it is now illegal to kill or maim any child or the family members of any child resulting from the coupling a witch and wolf. In addition, hybrids are afforded the same protections and rights as full-blooded witches and wolves. Minutes ago, Madame Adelia Wixx, head of one of the oldest

and largest witch clans in the world, named the hybrid Honey Smith, who also happens to be her great-granddaughter, as her successor. Madame Wixx claims to have evidence refuting the many charges laid against Honey and proposed that considering the great service Honey has done for all wolf and witch kind, that all charges be dropped. Madame Wixx's announcement appears to have caught many in the Wixx clan and in the larger witch community completely by surprise. Honey has not been sighted since her sudden reappearance in Scotland, where she purportedly broke the Curse of the Hybrids, and then in Indiana this past weekend. We will continue to bring you updates as the story unfolds."

Everyone turned to look at her, all with serious faces except Zavier. He shot her a crooked grin, "Madame Honey? It makes you sound like a fortune teller."

"Thanks."

"I wonder what the seer saw," Theo mused. She pushed off the counter and moved to the doorway to offer Honey her hand. "May I."

"I didn't realize your power works that way. I thought it was random."

"It usually is, but if the powers that be are actively trying to send a message or a warning, there is a chance I will pick up on it, especially if you are the subject and I am touching you."

Honey extended her hand, "Go for it."

Theo took Honey's hand and closed her eyes. A long moment passed before she opened them.

"What did you see?"

Instead of answering, Theo turned her head toward Lynn. As if on cue, the phone in Lynn's pocket began to ring. She

223

pulled it out to frown down at the screen, then tapped it and put it to her ear.

"Hello?"

"Hello Luna. I'm looking for Honey. Don't tell me if she's there, I just have a message for her."

Even from several feet away, Honey recognized her grandmother's soft voice.

"Rachel, why would you think she's with me?"

"It's more like you're one of the only wolves whose phone number I have. If you see her, could you tell her I need to speak with her? It's urgent."

"What has happened?" Lynn asked.

"Did you hear my mother's announcement?"

"I did."

"She needs to meet me where I saw her last."

Honey mouthed a 'why' toward Lynn who had turned to watch her.

"Why did your mom pick Honey?" Lynn asked. "Surely she could have picked someone less…controversial."

It was a good question but not the one Honey had meant and Lynn knew it.

"My mother holds her cards close to her chest but I think she's impressed not only with Honey's strength but also her determination to do what she believes is right. Also, of all the candidates my mother considered, Honey is the only one who didn't try and sweet-talk her to get her way. She hates that."

"What if Honey doesn't show up? What if she disappears for another year?" Lynn asked.

"Until she dies, she will always be the head of the Wixx clan. She needs to come here so the clan can protect her from those who would prefer someone else and so she can learn."

"What if she doesn't want the position?"

"Once it has been announced, it's not optional. The only ways to step down are by death or retirement and to retire, she must first pick her own successor, but only after my mother either steps down or passes away."

"What about Brayton." Lynn curled her lip. "They have a…thing."

"He should come too. As her consort, he's a target."

"Consort!?"

"It's what we witches call the spouses of our leaders. It's not official yet, but everyone knows he is with her and that makes him a target."

"He's a wolf. Surely it would be wiser and safer for him to stay with other wolves."

"Perhaps."

"No," Brayton said firmly.

"They are very young," her grandmother continued. *"If they were to go their separate ways for a while, it would give them both a chance to receive the schooling they need."*

Brayton was shaking his head so hard Honey was afraid he'd make himself dizzy.

"It makes sense," Honey sent. *"You could finish college with your friends. I will focus on learning magic."*

He leaned close enough that his whisper on her ear gave her goosebumps. "You are my mate and my Luna. I will not let you go."

His declaration touched her heart but there were so many obstacles. He wouldn't be able to go anywhere safely with her around. If she was gone though… "*Would it be so bad to separate for a while? We can still see each other,*" she added quickly when he started to protest, "*just secretly.*"

"If I see her, I'll pass on your message," Lynn said.

Honey grabbed Brayton's collar and pulled his lips to hers. "*This will work. You can get your life back on track and work things out with your mom. I'll learn about my witch side. It will give us time to decide how to go forward.*"

He pulled away from her but only so he could put his forehead against hers. "Is that what you want?" He transformed and sent, "*My life will be on track as long as I'm with you. We could focus on our own goals. We don't have to do everything together, but I don't think we should keep our relationship secret. People will accept it once they see we won't back down.*"

She transformed because, well, just because. "*But you will be in danger.*"

"*Maybe, but people will be less likely to harm me if the world is watching. Besides, you will be in more danger than me. Please, don't make me leave your side. I can't…Please.*"

"*Brayton…*"

"*I have never gotten hurt by your side. It was only when I was away from you that people burned me and tortured me and hurt you. Together we are strong. Together we can watch out for one another. Together we can learn about magic.*"

"*You want to learn magic?*"

He wiggled his wolfy eyebrows. "*You keep saying wolves have magic. We should test your theory. Marry me, Honey, the witch way. Right here, right now.*"

Her heart gave a strong thump that was almost painful. "*Here?*" It was too fast. She was barely sixteen. She had plans.

226

Plus, marriage was so…permanent, at least to her. Strictly speaking, the moon mating thing was much more so.

"*Honey. Look at me.*" Brayton used his paw to gently turn her head his way. "*I know you think we're too young – that you are too young, but after everything you've been through, I think you are more mature and have more experience than most people have at thirty. Trust me, I never imagined I'd feel this way about someone so soon either, but I can't picture myself without you. You are my other half. I want to be there with you. I want to rent an apartment with you and take turns cooking supper and go shopping together. That's right, I said shopping. You can go out with your friends whenever you want. I won't smother you. I just want to build the rest of my life with you. I want to be your family.*"

She already had family – her uncle/bio-dad and her grandmother and Zavier. She'd probably go live with her grandmother once it was safe to do so. She'd get to practice magic and read as many books in the library as she wanted to. If Brayton went back to his pack, she could get another pair of magic slates and write messages to him every night. Oh, wait, she didn't have to do that anymore. She could use phones now. It would be simpler to just pop in and talk to him though or maybe pull him to her. When had he become so integral in her life?

"*I can't picture my life without you either,*" she admitted. "*I suppose we can make it work.*"

"*Now?*"

"*Don't witches have special ceremonies?*"

His wolf grinned. "*All witches and wolves recognize ceremonies sanctioned by the legal system and all acting alphas are qualified to perform the ceremony and there are three in the room.*"

227

"What about a license?"

"I'm sure Zavier can take care of that."

"What about..." she started.

"We can wear our moon clothes. Theo can be the witness. Your brother can be the ring bearer, although wolves don't wear rings, for obvious reasons. Go get dressed. I'll take care of everything."

"What about your mom."

"What about her?"

"Look at her. She's clenching her hands so hard she's broken open her palms. She doesn't like me."

"She likes you just fine, she just feels guilty. Transform."

"Why?"

He touched her nose with his. "Trust me."

- *Brayton* -

He sure hoped this worked. As soon as Honey was in human form in front of him, he dropped to one knee.

"Honey you are the only woman for me. I love you and I want to make my life with you. Will you marry me here, in front of our families?"

"You know the answer."

He tilted his head toward their audience and mouthed, "They don't."

Honey eyes flickered toward their respective families then back to him with more panic than he'd ever seen on her normally calm face. Had she changed her mind? How could he convince her?

"Honey, it will be okay, I promise. No matter what they say, I am not leaving your side. I meant everything I said. Do you want to marry me?"

She gave a tiny nod followed by a faint 'yes,' then looked through her lashes at him with her beautiful green eyes. It took all his power to stay down on his knee and not sweep her into a kiss.

"*Will* you marry me?"

She bit her lip. He'd seen confident Honey, brave Honey, stubborn Honey, but that small sign of insecurity sealed his fate. No doubt every wolf and maybe even the witch in the room could smell his attraction.

Her nod was a little more confident this time. "Yes."

"*Now?*"

"YES!"

She barely had time to start laughing at his desperation before he was off his knees and kissing her.

"Ah-hem. There are innocent eyes present," someone said.

Brayton reluctantly pulled away to find all the male adults in the room looking at them in amusement while Honey's aunt/stepmom was glaring and holding her hand over Honey's cousin/brother's eyes and his own mom had her eyes closed. His grandfather handed a small booklet to Zavier.

"Thought this might come in handy."

"What is that?" Honey asked.

Zavier held it up. The couple saying their wedding vows on the cover looked like they were straight out of the 1960's. Zavier opened the book and flipped past the first few pages. "You want the long version or the short version?"

229

"Do they have the short-short version?" Honey asked.

"Are you in a hurry?" Brayton asked, amused.

"It was a reference – Space Balls – haven't you seen it?"

"No."

She grinned. "I know what we're watching on movie night."

"Wait."

He knew his mom was going to cause problems. "What Mom?"

"Don't you want to get married in front of your friends? What about your witch friends Honey?"

Honey's gaze traveled over everyone present. She stopped on Theo. "There's not enough room here for everyone, but I can think of one person who should be here. We'll be right back."

Brayton took a breath and pressed his lips together before she could warn him. Rolling her eyes, she pulled him into the nether with her, then pulled them back out into what looked like a cross between a garden shed, a laboratory, and a kitchen. It smelled strongly of herbs, probably due to the dry bunches hanging from the ceiling and the live ones in the window, but also of magic.

"Hi Grandma."

"Honey!" Mrs. Wixx grabbed her chest. "What are you… How did you get in here?"

Honey took her finger off the back of her grandmother's neck where she must have planted an anchor. "Are you busy?"

Mrs. Wixx looked down at the packets of seeds she appeared to be organizing. "No, not really."

"Would you like to come to a wedding?"

"Whose wedding?"

"Ours." Honey smiled at Brayton and squeezed his hand.

"When?"

"Right now."

"Now?"

Honey nodded, still grinning.

Brayton had never seen Mrs. Wixx so flustered. He wondered if she realized she was patting her seed packets.

"Oh. Well, let me get my coat and my purse. Stay here. I'll be right back."

"My mom told me about this room," Honey said, running her finger on the edge of the well-worn wooden table in the middle of the room after Mrs. Wixx hurried away. "This is where she learned how to make the candles and the teas she sold online and all about herbs." She released his hand and walked over to the small book stand in the corner where an old book was laying open. Honey gently touched the handwritten page. "My mom had a recipe book like this that she started when she was a little girl. It burned in the fire. I started one too but…"

Brayton pulled her to his shoulder when she started sobbing.

"Oh, my goodness. What happened?" Mrs. Wixx, now in a thick wool coat, asked from the doorway.

Before he could explain, an older, sharper voice came from somewhere beyond the door. "Rachel, have you heard anything yet?" The not-so-soft footsteps in the hallway got louder and the voice asked, "Rachel, do you feel that?" the steps came even closer. "It feels like...wolf! What is *he* doing here?"

Brayton wiggled his eyebrows at Madame Wixx who was now glaring at him from the door.

"Mother! They are...They just..." she looked at Brayton with wide eyes.

"We came to invite you to a wedding, Madame Wixx," Brayton blurted. "There will be lots of wolves though."

"A wedding?" She squinted at him. "Why is my great-granddaughter crying?"

He lifted a hand off Honey's back to point to the culprit. "It was the book, not me."

"And when is this wedding?"

"Now, well, as soon as we get back. Are you coming?"

To Brayton's shock, she started moving across the room toward them. "Yes."

"Mom, you need a coat."

"Is this wedding outside?"

"No," Brayton replied.

"Then I will be fine." She put her hand on Honey's shoulder. "Let's go."

Honey lifted her face from his shirt and wiped her cheeks. "Before we go, I should warn you that we're going to magically protected lands. If you attempt to harm or mean to harm anyone on the grounds, you will be ejected."

"Really?" Madame Wixx sounded more curious than concerned. "Are we going to visit your cousin then?"

"Yes."

"And we're traveling in this mysterious fashion that you've discovered?"

232

"Yes."

"Is it less discombobulating than a portal?"

"Just don't breathe."

Five seconds later they were back in the small house by the bathroom/bedroom doors where Honey must have planted an anchor.

"You weren't kidding about there being a lot of wolves," Madame Wixx said, looking regally around. She then turned on Honey. "Was that the nether?"

"Yes."

"You figured out how to use it to travel?"

"Yes."

Madame Wixx nodded. "I knew I was right about you. Do you know how many people have disappeared trying to figure that out?"

Honey scrunched her nose. "No, and I didn't really need to know." She shuddered. Brayton guessed that she, like he, was imagining all the bodies floating in the nether. Ew.

Madame Wixx turned around and took a deep breath. "Well, let's get on with it. Who has the ribbon?"

"What?" Honey asked.

"The ribbon. You've already been united in the wolf way. Since you are a hybrid, it makes sense that you should be united in the witch way as well." She put her open hand out to the side in front of her daughter. "Rachel?"

Honey's grandmother started digging in her over-sized purse. "I don't think I...oh. This should work." She pulled out a roll of medical tape and put it in her mother's hand. "Consider it sticky ribbon."

"What are you going to do with that?" Honey asked.

233

Her great-grandmother looked down her nose at Honey. "Bind your hands together, of course. You say your vows, and the magic will do the rest. Take each other's hands."

"Wait!" Theo said, pushing her way through everyone else from the corner of the room. "They must prepare."

"Who is this?" her great-grandmother frowned. "She is a witch."

"Theodosia Wixx, your great-great-great something-or-the-other," Honey grinned, "Theo, this is my great-grandmother, head of the Wixx coven."

"Blessed be, Mother," Theo curtsied.

"We use Madame now," Honey's great-grandmother corrected. "Honey, explain."

"She was trapped by a curse for over 200 years in the nether."

"That makes me the oldest witch here. I will perform the ritual," Theo proclaimed, "after they prepare, and with the appropriate materials. Alpha Zavier, can you please find a ribbon or cord made of natural materials long enough to tie around their hands?"

"My medical tape is of cotton," Mrs. Wixx proclaimed.

"Their wedding clothes were gifted by the moon. I think we can do better than that," Theo said sternly.

Ten minutes later, Honey and Brayton stood opposite one another, clothed in the glowing white moon garments, with their hands tied together with an organic silk ribbon that Zavier had procured from somewhere. Brayton's insides had never felt so tight and oddly mushy at the same time.

The moon ceremonies had been just as binding, but unexpected. This they had chosen. This, Honey had chosen. She was *choosing* to be with him. She was choosing *him*.

"Repeat after me," Zavier said, reading from the scrap of paper inserted inside Grandpa's book. Theo, standing in front of Zavier with her hands above and below his and Honey's, looked expectantly at Brayton. He didn't need Zavier's prompting to recite the lines he and Honey had hastily edited to make the vows fit their situation.

"I, Brayton Maxwell Mooney, take you, Honey Smith, my love and my moon-chosen mate to be my wife and queen, to love and cherish, in the good times and the bad, in sickness and in health, as long as I shall live, according to God's will."

A tear dripped from the corner of Honey's eye when she started speaking

"I, Honey Smith, daughter of Madeline Wixx and Matthias Silver, take you (sniff), Brayton Maxwell Mooney, my love and moon-chosen mate (sniff) to be my husband and consort, to love and cherish, in the good times and the bad, in sickness and in health, as long as I shall live, according to God's will."

"By the powers that be," Theo and Zavier said in unison.

"I proclaim you alpha and luna," Zavier said alone.

"Witch and her chosen," Theo said.

"Husband and wife," they said together. "What God has joined let no one tear asunder."

"So mote it be," Theo said and abruptly removed her hands from theirs and the ribbon wrapped around it.

The ribbon started to glow, then to slither around their hands like it was slipping off, then vanished.

"Where did it go?" Brayton asked.

"Theo?" Honey asked with concern.

Theo's eyes had gone white again. Brayton grabbed Honey's hand. No one was going to snatch her away ever again.

Theo blinked, then turned her now normal eyes toward his parents. "By accepting a witch into your midst, the curse on the Mooney family is broken. Your womb is free of the shackles that bound it."

"What?" his mother sputtered.

"In answer to your question, Brayton, look at your wrist," Theo smiled at him like nothing abnormal had just happened.

It was faint, but he could see the outline of the ribbon on his skin, slightly lighter than the rest of his skin. Honey had a mark too.

"You may kiss the bride," Zavier said.

Tears still dotted Honey's cheeks. Brayton reached up and wiped them away with his thumb, then placed a gentle kiss on her lips before pulling her into his arms. He was pretty sure she was thinking about her parents.

"Do you think they approve?" he whispered.

She nodded and after a moment put her face up toward his with a sly, shy smile.

Grinning, he obliged her silent request.

27

BRAYTON – SIX MONTHS LATER – ROME

"How do I look?" Brayton spun around in the tux Honey's Grandmother had laid on their bed.

"I like the bow tie," Honey grinned.

He sauntered across the hotel room to stand beside her in front of the mirror. She looked like a young movie star with her short hair all styled and her formal attire but that wasn't the kind of compliment she liked. "You should. It matches your dress."

"Why is it I have to dress like this," she waved her hand over the one-strap, floor-length flowing red dress, "While you get to wear that? There's not enough room in this thing to take a full step."

"The dress looks a lot better on you."

"You think?"

He ran a finger over her exposed collar bone, "and it allows me to do this."

"Brayton."

He could no more resist the heated look she gave him then a starving dog could resist a slab of meat. He put his hands on her satin-covered hips and pulled her to his lips.

"Hey! You guys ready?" Giselle called through the door. Before either of them had time to answer or even step out of the kiss, the door lock clicked open and Giselle barged into the room.

Brayton managed one last peck on Honey's lips before she stepped away. He glared at Giselle over Honey's shoulder, but the deceptively young-looking woman didn't notice, like always. Having spent the majority of her fifty-five years as a two-year-old had left Giselle somewhat oblivious to social clues and norms, like not barging in on newly married couples in a fancy hotel room, or anywhere. Honey was, of course, good friends with her.

Giselle clapped her hands together. "Oh, you look fantabulous!"

"You think?" Honey said. "I was thinking maybe we got the outfits wrong. Don't you think this dress would look better on him?"

Giselle scrutinized Honey's dress and then Brayton as if Honey was serious. "I don't think it would fit around his chest. But it would look interesting. You should have him try it on after the dinner."

Honey observed him speculatively. "Maybe I will."

He had never ever considered wearing a dress before, but the mischievous glint in her eye had him considering it. Perhaps it would make a good kilt.

A small male, not wolf, knocked on the open door. "Pardon me, is one of you Honey Wixx?

"That would be me," Honey said.

"This was delivered for you at the front desk." He held out a letter and started to walk into the room.

"Stop right there. I'll take that," Giselle said, whipping the envelope out of his fingers.

"Thank you." Honey said to the man who had bowed and was rapidly backing his way out the door.

Brayton shut it behind him.

"It just has your name on it," Giselle said. She shook the envelope, then put it on the small table by the door and backed away. Brayton smelled Giselle's magic just before the envelope tore and a folded piece of paper floated into the air.

"Nothing blew up," she commented.

"Always a good sign," Honey snorted.

Brayton stepped closer to sniff the paper. "I don't see any magic but it smells weird, like some kind of animal."

Honey stepped beside him and sniffed it herself, then grabbed the piece of paper out of the air and unfolded it and held it so Brayton could read it over her shoulder.

Dear Miss American Pie,

You may not remember us, as you were having memory problems at the time, but we would love to meet with you again while you are here in Rome. Ever since she met you, one of our mutual acquaintances has been suffering from an identity crisis which we believe you might be able to help with. If you would be amenable to a meeting, please leave a message at the email on the bottom of the page. We will compensate you for your time.

Distiniti Saluti
C.

"Miss American Pie?" Brayton asked.

"Yeah. It's from those people who kidnapped me the last time I was in Rome."

"You were kidnapped?" Giselle asked with surprise.

"My escape attempt didn't go as planned. They dropped me on my head and I lost my memory for a while. They wanted to make some ransom money off me but I couldn't remember my name, so their plan didn't work out, not that it would have if I could have remembered my name."

"And they have the nerve to ask you to meet with them?" Giselle scoffed.

"How did they know you were here? Are they witches?" Brayton asked. Honey had never said much about it, but he'd had the impression they were wolves.

"No, but I'm certain they associate with some." Honey glanced at the hotel alarm clock. "We have ten minutes. That's time enough if we go down now."

"You aren't going to reply, are you," Giselle asked before Brayton could.

Honey shrugged. "I'm curious. I don't think they'll hurt me. They have no reason to."

"Hello. You are basically witch royalty. Now they have even more reason to try and make some ransom money off you."

Brayton nodded in agreement.

"Don't worry. I'll take precautions. Brayton will too."

"You're going to take me?" Brayton asked, slipping his arms around her from behind and leaning his chin on her shoulder because.

"Of course. Otherwise, you will nag me incessantly."

"True." She'd gotten much better at including him in things, in fact she rarely did anything without him. He could have done without some of the meetings with the local coven leaders, but he was glad to be there because then he knew she was safe.

She slipped on her dainty, high-heeled shoes, which he knew from experience would end up in the nether as soon as she sat down, then charged out of the room and toward the elevator. It took her barely two minutes to send a short reply from a temporary email address she quickly set up in an incognito window, then they were off to the annual world witch's ball.

This was the third annual witch ball he'd attended, although it was the first world one. Of one thing he was certain. It was going to be an awful night. Witches did not know how to party. Fancy dress and multiple courses meant you had to sit for hours and try and find something to talk about with the strangers around you, when they would deign to talk to a wolf, while trying not to sweat through your jacket. The dancing was even worse. A song had to be at least 100-years-old before they would play it.

Mrs. Wixx was waiting for them in the grand foyer outside the hallway that led to the dining room wearing the fanciest dress he'd seen her in so far. This one had pale flowers all over it that she'd accessorized with pearls, long white gloves, and a delicate pearl tiara that peeked out of her white hair.

"You look lovely Grandmother," Brayton said.

"Oh, stop."

"He's right," Honey said. "And the blush adds the perfect touch of color."

Mrs. Wixx's cheeks got even pinker and she shook her head. "You two. I'm too old to blush. Mother has already been announced and is making her rounds. I'll go in before you like we've done before. At this level, any attacks are more likely to be sneak than direct but as always, keep your eyes open and watch your backs."

"And she wonders why we didn't seem excited about attending," Brayton mumbled behind Mrs. Wixx's back.

Mrs. Wixx stopped and looked back over her shoulder. "Don't give me that. I know for a fact you two like a good fight. I've seen you practicing. You just don't like the way all the eligible young men flock to Honey's side."

"She's got you there," Honey said near his ear.

"Like you are any better when it comes to the women."

"At least I don't growl at them."

"No, you just freeze them."

"Only when they get annoying."

Mrs. Wixx sent them a stern 'Behave!' look over her shoulder then stepped forward to be announced. Brayton half-expected the guards by the door to bar their way for being wolves like they had at the first ball, but the ones here pretended they didn't notice. Perhaps that was due to the strong anti-wolf ward his magical eye was picking up over the entrance.

"*I smell lightning and gunpowder. It will undoubtedly go off when we break the ward,*" Honey warned.

"Guess they wanted to make sure everyone noticed our entrance," he mumbled. "How kind of the organizers."

"*Indeed.*" Out loud she said, "Giselle, go protect my grandmother."

"I'm supposed to be *your* guard."

"Please. We're about to make a big entrance. Make sure she's clear of the door."

"What are you going to do?"

"You'll see."

Honey let the people behind them go first. Once they were clear, his magic eye spied a shape like a bent shield shoot from Honey toward the center of the wide doorway, then his view was blocked by a small cinder-block wall. The resulting explosion was louder than he expected, and definitely not expected by the people who had just joined the queue behind them. Honey's wall kept them all safe from flying debris, and the stiff breeze afterward quickly cleared the dust, leaving them clean, albeit wind-blown.

Honey brushed off her dress, then reached up and brushed her fingers through his hair. "How do I look?"

He couldn't help himself. He planted a kiss in the center of the faint spot on her forehead, making in glow even brighter.

"Perfect." He waved his hand at the wall, "Where did that come from?"

"The shed that lost its roof in the windstorm. Theo told me it might come in useful to have a solid barrier."

"Huh."

She flashed him a grin and sent the wall back to the nether, then strode confidently forward into the now much bigger doorway. If whoever had put up the ward meant for them to grab everyone's attention when they arrived, they'd succeeded.

The eyes of the dusty, disheveled attendant widened, and a faint look of fear crossed his features right before he ducked his head into a bow.

"M-Mistress Wixx."

"Wixx-Moon," Honey corrected. "Please announce my consort and me. Don't forget to mention he's an alpha."

"O-of course," the attendant croaked.

"Are you ever going to get tired of calling me that?" Brayton asked, stepping to her side and taking her hand.

"What? Alpha?"

"Very funny."

During their introduction, his magic eye registered movement along the edges of the room. He couldn't see through the invisibility shields, but from the shapes he was certain at least twenty people were about to invisibly converge on them. "I thought your grandmother said the challenges would be more subtle here."

"I guess she was wrong. You want to take this one?"

"You don't want to let your wolf side out?"

"I don't think we should reveal all our strengths right off the bat, plus I like this dress."

"Fair enough." He focused on the shapes slinking around the walls and sent out a strong 'Sleep' command.

There were some charms, namely the ones Honey made, that could protect against his enhanced alpha power, but whoever the secret ninjas were, they didn't have them. They all fell where they were, some knocking into people and tables and other simply rolling behind the furniture.

"I wonder if they'll realize that was you?" Honey sent.

He shrugged in reply, earning him a little half-grin. Man, he loved this woman.

The caped witches who were purportedly providing security for the conference finally realized there was a problem and started responding to the screams of the people by the walls. Brayton used the distraction to escort Honey through the middle of the dining room toward her family who were seated on the opposite side of the room.

Madame Wixx greeted them like nothing odd was happening at all while Mrs. Wixx's eyes kept flickering from them to the action.

"No one's hurt," Brayton informed her.

"Do you know what's going on?"

Conscious of the man on Mrs. Wixx's left who was leaning closer with his ear up in the air, Brayton shrugged. "From where we were, it looked like some chairs fell over. I'm sure if they need a healer they'll come and get you."

She nodded and relaxed back into her seat a fraction. "Yes, yes, you're right of course."

An attendant directed Honey to the seat on Madame Wixx's right. Brayton took the only remaining seat which was, thankfully, next to Honey's.

Brayton leaned forward to address Madame Wixx. "I take it from your casual attitude that this is normal?"

The old lady gave him a lazy look. "I've seen a lot. I can't imagine this is tamer than a wolf conference with your excitable natures."

"We usually don't have exploding wards or invisible ninjas."

"Is that what they are?"

"I'm guessing."

A good thirty minutes later, the servers finally brought out the first plates of food. There were three items on his plate. They looked pretty, but only the smallest one appeared to be meat and it was pink and sliced so thin he could see through it. He took a sniff and grabbed Honey's arm.

"Do you smell that?"

She lowered the upside-down mushroom filled with something that wasn't meat from her mouth.

"What?"

"It smells like sulfur."

She sniffed the air and looked around. "There's smoke coming out of the bottom of the food carts, thick smoke."

"Smoke bombs?" he suggested.

"Maybe. I don't smell any magic, but it is getting hard to see in here." He smelled her magic and the smoke started to all flow towards the walls.

"We should leave," Sharon, Madame Wixx's guard, said behind Madame Wixx.

"Erect a shield, but let's stay and see who's behind this and what they want," Madame Wixx instructed calmly.

Sharon tossed a charm on the floor. A half-sphere of magic burst out, forming a barrier between their group and everyone around them. All along the table similar bubbles popped into existance.

"Is this strong enough to keep out non-magical objects?" Honey asked.

"Yep," Sharon responded. "You could be in point-blank range of a bomb and come out unscathed."

"But it lets magic out?"

"Yeah, and bullets if you have a gun. It's one-way protection."

"Wow."

"What about poison?" he asked.

"Safe," Sharon confirmed.

"And air?" Honey asked.

"Recycled. Ten people can stay inside for up to twelve hours."

"How do you take it down?" Honey asked.

"Tap the charm."

Honey turned to Madame Wixx. "I want to learn how to make one of these next."

"I suspected you would."

The smoke dissipated. The servants slowly started reappearing to collect their carts. The witch who was in charge of the proceedings stepped into the middle of the tables proclaiming all was well, nothing dangerous had been found, and that it was all apparently a prank.

"Take down the shield," Madame Wixx ordered.

"Whoever sent the smoke could be waiting for that," Sharon protested.

"We can't stay in here forever."

"Let Brayton and I check it out," Honey said. We can smell if there's anything to be concerned about in the air. I assume we can just walk out of the shield?"

"Yes, but you won't be able to get back in once you are fully out."

"Understood."

Honey moved to the edge of the shield and stuck her face out. "This feels weird. I don't smell anything off, except the sulfur, and it's fading."

Brayton followed her lead and took a sniff for himself. The scent of magic from all the shields, plus whatever spells the other witches had tried on the smoke was overwhelming, but none of it smelled inherently bad. He said as much.

"Drop the shield. Show people the American Wixxes aren't afraid," Madame Wixx directed.

As soon as their shield dropped, the other shields started to vanish. Ten minutes later the servants brought out the second course.

The rest of the evening went smoothly. A steady stream of people dropped by to speak to Madame Wixx during the dancing and were subsequently introduced to him and Honey, but no one tried to coax her away. Maybe the explosion had been just the deterrent they needed.

"Pardon," an attendant said after everyone had been dancing at least an hour. "I have a message for Mistress Wixx."

Giselle took the envelope from him and thanked him with a flirtatious smile and a wink. The poor man was so distracted, he turned around and nearly collided right into a passing waiter. Giselle laughed and handed the envelope to Honey.

Honey sniffed it, then opened the letter.

"Who is it from?" Madame Wixx enquired.

Honey handed the short note to Brayton. All it said was "*I am here. Come alone.*"

"A prior acquaintance. I need to take care of this. Brayton, you want to come? We should be back in a few minutes, no more than half-an-hour."

"Be careful," Madame Wixx demanded.

"I will."

"The note said to come alone," Brayton pointed out once they were out of hearing range of her family.

"Do you want me to go by myself?"

"No. I was just surprised I didn't have to argue with you."

"I don't trust them but if it's something I caused and I can fix, then I feel like I should."

"What did you do?"

"Defended myself. Called a bluff which was probably not a bluff at all. I don't know. I need to see what they say."

"Okay. You know I have your back."

She slipped her hand into his, "I know."

"Where are we going?"

"To the lobby."

She smiled at the people they passed while skirting the dance floor, but didn't engage with any of them, nor did any engage with her. He could feel the eyes of everyone in the room on their backs though, especially when it became obvious they were going to step out of the room. Why? Was there another trap? Other people were coming and going.

She turned her deceptively calm aka fighting face on him and his heartbeat ratcheted up a few beats. "Get your alpha power ready and be prepared to dodge."

"I thought we were going to the lobby."

"We are. Hold your breath."

- *Honey* -

If someone had told her a year ago that she would marry Brayton Mooney of all people, she would have checked their heads to see if their molecules were scrambled. Now she couldn't imagine being without him, which was why there was no way she was going to leave him behind, not with those crazy shapeshifters around. Plus, they worked better together. They belonged together. Even his mother could see it, although her continued insistence that they move back onto pack lands was getting old. Maybe she'd calm down once she had the baby, which Honey was pretty sure was going to happen since Lynn was past the third month and the curse that had limited Brayton's family to one baby a generation was gone.

The murk of the nether surrounded them. Honey pulled the old sailing ship to them, then used her magic sight to locate the magically protected shield she'd stashed for emergencies and handed it to Brayton. A moment later, they were standing behind the public computer in the little room just off the main lobby where she'd planted an anchor hours before.

"A shield?" Brayton whispered. "Where did you get this?"

"From the library at school," she sent.

"Ms. Cummings let you take it?"

"The library did."

"You are brave. Is that who we are meeting?"

He nodded to the girl dressed all in black who was standing in the center of the lobby expectantly watching the hallway that led toward the dining room.

Honey nodded. As she'd suspected, Carmela hadn't come alone either. Several darkly clothed people waited on either side of the hall doorway and others crouched behind chairs and beside the main desk. There were no witches standing anywhere, although several were laying down side-by-side on the floor. Honey hoped they were only sleeping.

"Put them all to sleep except the woman in the middle. Stay close to me. I've put an air shield around both of us so they can't smell us coming."

Brayton squeezed her hand, then she felt his power shoot through the room. The people around the doorway abruptly relaxed and slid down the wall to fall over on each other. Others fell out from behind the furniture. More than she expected slid down from the ceiling, although the ropes they were attached to prevented them from falling completely.

"This is crazy," Brayton whispered into her ear. "Who are these people?"

"Roman mafia with a magic twist."

Carmela's sharp gaze scanned the lobby and eventually pinpointed their location. She raised her eyebrows as if to say "Really?"

Honey smiled and waved, then waited for Carmela to walk to them. She wasn't about to lose the advantage the enclosed room afforded them over the wide-open lobby. Nor was she going to let the girl get close to Brayton with some of those nasty charms she was wearing. Honey tore through the protection charms and froze Carmela's limbs when they were in a comfortable speaking distance.

Carmela abruptly realized she couldn't lift her foot and gave a bemused shake of her head. "You froze me again, didn't you?"

"Yep."

"And you didn't come alone."

"Neither did you."

"True, although to be fair," she tilted her head toward the foyer, "that wasn't me. I really did just want to have a conversation."

"You found my clue."

"Si."

"Then what's the problem?"

Carmela's eyes flickered to Brayton.

"Oh, this is Brayton, my consort."

"Mate," he corrected.

"He hates it when I call him consort," Honey grinned.

"I know who he is," Carmela said. "You'd have to live under a rock not to."

"You pretty much do, or did you move?"

"Ha ha, funny. You know why I can't speak in front of him, or did you tell him?"

"I did not. Just tell me, which acquaintance were you referring to?"

"Annia."

"Does it have anything to do with the shot?"

"No. It's what you did to all of us. Remember how she could only partially transform because you froze her?"

"Yes."

252

"Well, now when she transforms either her head is human or her body is human, but not both."

She didn't need Brayton's hand-squeeze to know the girl was lying, but Honey decided to play along.

"So, she's like those Egyptian gods with the animal heads."

"Don't even put that idea into her head."

Honey laughed. "Where is she now?"

"In a van, waiting for me to bring you."

"Is she the one behind the ninjas?"

"Yep."

"Was she also responsible for the gas that was coming through the vents?"

"That was Gaio."

"Lovely. And is Gaio even now attempting to capture my grandmas so that she can have leverage over me?"

"Probably."

Honey was doubly glad she'd made them both anti-everything protection charms, not that they needed them with all the charms her family had made and collected over the years. "She doesn't need leverage. I'd be glad to help."

"You would?"

"Sure. I didn't mean to do that to her."

"Then you'll come with me?"

"Absolutely not. Here."

Honey scribbled a swirly symbol that humans tended to associate with witches on a complementary post-it note and stuck it on Carmela's still-frozen body. "Stick this to her back – her shirt preferably, then send a text to this number," she wrote down the # to her new cell phone on another note and stuck it next to the first one, "and I'll fix her."

"You can do that?"

Honey shrugged. "In theory. You can text again if it doesn't work. Also, when you send the text, tell her to hold her breath."

"Why?"

"It's safer."

Brayton touched her elbow at the same time she smelled the portal opening. There was a slight chance it was a friend, but she highly doubted it. Besides, Brayton had already halted the portal's formation with his eye. Honey pulled the shed wall back from the nether just as whatever he'd caught midway through the portal entrance exploded with a muffled boom. Only a few pieces of plaster pelleted them, but she was certain there was some major damage somewhere.

She froze Carmela completely and proceeded to destroy every remaining magical and technological item on her, including the earpiece she discovered hiding behind her ear.

"They must be the ones who sent that bomb to the library, and I'll bet Annia is fine. I'm not the only witch who can freeze people," Honey said, looking Carmela up and down for anything she'd missed.

"I was wondering about that," Brayton confessed, both watching her and keeping watch around them.

"I was giving her the benefit of the doubt because I wasn't sure how easily they could find a witch with the right skills. Nice job with the portal, by the way."

"My pleasure."

Honey stopped in front of Carmela and studied her frozen face. "Do you think Carmela knew she was the sacrificial bait?"

"Only she could tell you that."

"Indeed."

Honey sent the wall back to the nether than grabbed Brayton's hand and Carmilla's frozen arm. A few moments later, they were in standing in a dark, chilly cave. Honey pulled her stashed backpack from the nether and pulled out a head lamp that she offered to Brayton with a kiss on his cheek before slipping one on her own head. That earned her a close embrace and a much nicer kiss that nearly made her forget there was someone in the cave with them. Brayton must have remembered though because Carmela was still standing like a dark statue when he ended the toe-curling kiss with a smaller one to her nose and gently spun her around to face Carmela. She tapped on her headlight and refroze Carmela's body but not her head.

"Was killing me Gaio's primary or secondary objective?" Honey asked.

"Where are we?" Carmela asked.

"Answer my question and I'll answer yours."

"Secondary."

"But you knew there was a good chance you could die?"

"You didn't answer my question."

"Australia."

"Yes. Why are we here?"

"Because they just tried to sacrifice you to get revenge for something they'd already fixed. Do you truly want to stay with those people? You can stay here and start a new life if you want."

"I can't just…"

"Yes, you can. I'll help you."

"Why?"

That was a good question. Carmela had no reason at all to trust her.

"Because I don't like to see people trapped."

"What would I do?"

Honey shrugged. "Whatever you want. Get a job, make friends, go to school, hitchhike across the continent."

"What about my," she paused, "pack?"

Did cats require pack bonds too? Honey hadn't sensed any bond-like scent on her. "Do you need one? If your leader thinks you're dead, will she bother severing ties?"

"No, I meant my friends – the ones you've met."

It was bad enough she was letting Carmela loose by herself. She could just imagine the damage her two friends could do.

"Are they safe for now?"

"They should be. Gaio mostly blamed me for what happened to Annia since she considers me the responsible one."

"Everything that happened was Annia's fault," Honey couldn't keep herself from pointing out. "Did she get sick from whatever it was she tried to inject me with?"

Brayton's hand tightened on her own. He didn't like recalling all the things she'd lived through while she was alone. Her heart melted a little like it always did when he did something sweet and she squeezed his hand back.

"Sí. It was bad."

"I thought she was bluffing about a poison. It smelled like salt."

"No, it was a virus isolated from wolves, animal wolves," Carmela clarified. "They were going to see if it worked against werewolves but Annia showed that it works against," her eyes flicked toward Brayton, "...against the cure they thought they had."

"But she thought I was a witch."

"Yes, but they wanted to test it on a witch and humans too before they used it. Gaio wanted the wolves out of the way, not the humans or the witches. Annia was trying to impress her by killing two birds with one stone."

"Is Annia better now?"

"Health-wise, sí, but Rome will never be a safe place for you."

"Great," Honey sighed, not that she was planning to visit Rome that often. She switched back to the more important topic at hand. "We can work together to get your friends out, but you should establish yourself first with a legal job and a place to stay. That way they'll have a safe place to come to and won't be tempted to kidnap anyone."

"Sure. I'll do that," Carmela rolled her eyes.

"Your confidence is overwhelming."

This wasn't going to work unless Carmela wanted it. How could she convince her to try? Honey pulled her old backpack out of the nether again and put it on backwards so she could dig through it. "We're a couple of miles from Sydney. There are a lot of hikers that go by but there are also wolves or something like wolves so you'll want to be careful. I broke your charm, but I have something that will help."

Honey pulled a smaller bag out of the pocket of her backpack containing all the charms she'd made and collected. The disguise charm Grandma's friend had given her so long ago fell into her hand. Should she give it to Carmela? Would it even still work? There was no reason for the girl to go anywhere near the Boston library, but if what Honey suspected was true – namely that she'd been gifted the charm only to encourage her to go to Boston, not because she truly needed to use it, it wouldn't matter if Carmela had it. She started to offer the charm to Carmela, but something stopped her. She dropped it back inside the bag and held up a charm shaped like a turtle instead.

"This is an air shield. It will hide your scent from everyone. Witches will still be able to sense your furriness though, so they'll assume you are a wolf." Honey hooked the charm's jump ring around the orange hairband she'd also pulled out. "The hairband will protect you from scrying and portal bombs and basically anyone who wants to find you. I also added a protection charm." She grinned up at Carmela's confused face. "It works against death charms, but if you smell burnt sugar, run."

"Right," Carmela said, wiggling her thawing shoulders. "Why are giving me these?"

"Would you rather I leave you with nothing? Let's see," Honey dug deeper into the bag. "Here are a couple of cash cards. Should be $500 on each. Oh, and, you know how to drive, right?"

"Sí, why?"

Honey pulled out the ID-maker she'd found in the small library at her grandmother's house and held it up. "Smile. Oh, no wait, you need a better background. Stand over there, against the wall."

"Why?"

"So I can take your picture for your ID."

"What?"

Honey snapped the picture. The ID-maker immediately started spitting out a license. Honey grabbed it just as it shot out. "Ooo, that's a nice name – Grace Harris. You're 22 and you live in New South Wales. Here."

"That…you got me with my mouth open."

Honey shrugged. "Makes it look more realistic, doesn't it. Here's your passport."

Honey handed the fresh booklet to Carmela and the ID-maker to Brayton so she could pull out the sweats stuffed in the bottom of the bag.

"I think these are clean. Do you want them?"

"No. I don't want your clothes. I have my own clothes."

"They aren't here though." Honey stuffed the clothes back into her pack. She was making a huge assumption – mainly that Carmela actually wanted to leave her pack. "Do you want to go back? I can take you back if you want."

"They are my friends. I can't just abandon them."

"I know how your feel. I had friends I had to leave behind when I was on the run. They are still my friends and they understood." She wasn't sure how she'd manage it, but she asked anyway, "If you could leave with them, would you?"

"It's impossible. We are tied to the Claw from birth. They own us."

"Would the Claw come after you here?"

"Nowhere is safe."

"Even if they don't know you're here? I've given you protection charms and a new identity and I removed everything magical and disabled all the non-magical items on you. As long as you avoid cameras and calling people with your phone, there's no reason they should find you, plus there's a good chance you blew up."

"No. They'll know I didn't. They always recover the bodies even if there's not much left."

"Bodies?" Brayton asked.

Carmela raised an eyebrow at him.

"Maybe they'll think I captured you," Honey suggested after pondering the problem for a moment. "Would they attempt a rescue?"

"Gaio wouldn't, not an American soil, but my friends might."

"Really? That would be perfect. Then I could capture them too and send them to you."

Carmela blinked at her like she'd just said the Earth was flat, then shook her own head before studying all the things Honey had stuffed in her hand. "Nothing is free. What do you want out of this?"

"I don't want anything. I know what it's like to be in a tough situation and you seem like someone who would benefit from a little help."

"Don't lie."

"I'm not and you know it. However," she truly hadn't even considered it until that moment, but if it would convince Carmela to stay and at least try for a while…"If you really

260

want to do something, there is a one thing you could look into for me."

"I knew it."

"You totally don't have to, but if you want to, there was a human, Arthur Helman, who let me stay in his house for a while. I was blamed for his murder, but it happened long after I was gone, about a year ago actually. He claimed his daughter, who is a cop by the way, wanted him out of the house, but I think she really cared for him. I just want to know if he was truly murdered and if so, why?"

"And if I did look into this for you, how would I contact you if I'm not supposed to use my phone?"

It was dangerous giving Carmela a way to contact her, but she had a good point. Honey pulled the slim case full of business cards her grandmother had gifted her out of the front of the backpack. Instead of her name, three iridescent stars were printed across the center.

"Place the card with the three stars touching your forehead and I'll come to you. Make sure there's room for me to land."

"And do not use it to harm her or with intentions to harm or turn her in or expose her or turn against her for any traitorous reason," Brayton added. "You can only use it if you truly need to talk with her and mean her no harm. And do not give it or let anyone else take it to use either."

Carmela released a gasp like she'd been hit. "What was that?"

"*Good thinking,*" Honey sent to Brayton along with a hand squeeze, then said aloud, "His alpha power. It works on witches too."

261

Carmela frowned like she wanted to argue that she was neither wolf nor witch, but finally nodded. "Handy."

"It is," Honey agreed.

"Okay, I'll stay and figure out who murdered the old man."

"Thank you."

Honey turned to Brayton, accidentally blinding him with her headlight. Oops. "What do you think? Shall we do an extraction or return to the party?"

Brayton scrunched his nose, "Better go to the party. Madame is probably waiting for us, and you know what she said about your portals."

"Right." Honey resisted the urge to look at Carmela and see how she responded to Brayton's insinuation that they'd used a portal to get here. She might buy it if she'd never used one before. As far as Honey knew, no one had yet realized she was using the nether and her grandmothers weren't telling.

"Gaio might be waiting," Carmela cautioned.

"Even though she bombed us?" Honey asked.

"She went to a lot of effort to infiltrate the witch's ball. She'll have had more than one goal. Probably something to do with inciting the witches against the local packs."

"Won't that affect your pack as well," Brayton asked.

"Not if it looks like we weren't involved."

"Would she harm anyone? Other than us I mean?" Honey asked.

"I doubt she'd kill all the witches. That would attract too much attention, but there are a few local ones she might target."

Brayton squeezed Honey's hand. "We better go then."

"Let's disguise ourselves, so they don't know it's us."

"I'm pretty sure they will know…." Carmela began.

Honey grinned at the way Carmela's mouth fell open when her red dress turned into an all-black, loosely fitting uniform not unlike that of a highly trained enforcer. It came complete with a magical mask that distorted and darkened her features, making identification impossible without the aid a powerful magical-see through device like Brayton's eye. Beside her, Brayton tapped the cuff-link that matched Honey's bracelet to magic on his own, matching uniform. She waved at Carmela, then dragged Brayton with her into the nether.

NOTES FROM THE AUTHOR

You made it to the end! Thanks for reading. If you enjoyed the story, please leave a review and tell your friends and your librarian. (Seriously, I have no patience for marketing and word of mouth is probably the only way people will hear about this).

This is the third series I've written. The Rabiah series and the Royal series are both available online in the normal places. I'm learning as I go, so if you check out those series, please excuse the not-so-great covers. My real life inspiration for Honey is on one of them, although they don't look alike, so I haven't talked myself into changing them yet.

Peace and Blessings and have a wonderful, wonderful day.

www.ingramcontent.com/pod-product-compliance
Lightning Source LLC
Chambersburg PA
CBHW022155170626
46807CB00005B/2218